IT TAKES WATER

A Novel

Susan Olupitan

Cover design by Jacqueline Tam

ISBN: 1983427225
ISBN 13: 9781983427220

For my mother, Ursel Berek Olupitan.
If I were to say all that I want to,
it would fill a whole other book.
So suffice it to say;
I am, because you are.

TABLE OF CONTENTS

PROLOGUE

1993

"But why does she have to go through all my stuff? I told her I would do it myself this weekend. It's not like the decorator is coming in *to-day*! I hate it when she does that. She can be so impatient."

"Forgive her, Beth. That's how mothers are. You may be like that too one day." said the calm amused voice of Calvert Lambeau on the other end.

"Grrrr! You are always being so accommodating. I bet you'd be different if she were your mom."

"I just keep my mind on better things, that's all."

"Uh-huh, yeah, right!"

"Like right now, I'm too excited about tonight to be bothered by your mother supposedly invading your privacy."

"So why don't you just tell me about this secret place you're taking me. Maybe then I could be excited too."

"But then it wouldn't be a surprise anymore. Gotta go. I'll pick you up at four."

"Babe, you know I get off at five."

"Better come up with a really good excuse then. You've got enough time to think of one. Bye!"

"Cal!? . . ." he had hung up. *What was he up to?*, she wondered. You just never knew with Cal.   One time he had surprised her with a dinner date at Popeye's. They'd laughed for hours afterwards, but when she'd told her friends about it, they didn't quite share the humor.

Nonetheless, that was one thing she loved about him, his spark and spontaneity. Another was his smoldering good looks. He stood a strapping six foot tall, his complexion was 'dark chocolate' which was what she called him in many an intimate moment. His body was solid muscle and standing before you, he emanated a stalwart strength demonstrating his disciplined dedication to the care of his physique. His full lips were bordered by a narrow mustache that added to his twenty-seven years an air of mature elegance softened by his deep dark brown eyes shaded by lashes that Beth felt she would be eternally envious of. The third thing that sealed the deal for her was his smarts. They had met in a political science class in College. As partners on a research project, they had a lot of time to spend together and get to know each other. It was their discovered common ground that attracted him to her months after she had already declared her undying love for him, albeit only in her mind. He had been voted the most eligible bachelor in their senior year. She never thought she'd stand a chance against the many runway-worthy ladies that made their intentions clear to him even in her presence, so she was pleasantly surprised when he first asked her out. Not that she was ever short of admirers herself, but none of them was Calvert Lambeau III.

She picked up the folder she was working on and tried to focus.

Bethany, an effervescent twenty-six year old, complimented his height at five foot four inches. She wore her full brown hair straight and long. Her large eyes mirrored her dark hair adding contrast to her light brown skin while her lips formed a perfect pink frame for her sparkling teeth when she smiled. He called her beautiful, but she was not so convinced. Somewhere inside herself she still prepared herself for the day that he would leave her for someone taller, sexier and more beautiful.

At four on the dot, he was there. She had not come up with an excuse but had told her supervisor that she wished to leave early for a 'hot date'.

"Yes, he *is* hot, isn't he?" her supervisor had smiled. "You'd better hold on tight to that one."

"A taxi?" she asked surprised. "What happened to your car?"

"Well, I thought arriving in a taxi would look classier."

Classier? she thought to herself. So it couldn't be Popeye's this time. Hopefully she was appropriately dressed for whatever was in store.

A half hour later, they arrived at the Airport. He rushed her in and straight to the security line.

"What the devil is going on, Cal? I am not going a step further."

"Oh, but you are going *so much* further."

She was getting angry now, "Cal!!!"

"Remember my Dad's friend, Xavier, the archeologist?" She nodded and he went on excitedly,

"Well, he's invited us to visit a research site he is working on... in..." he held up the flight tickets for her to see "...Egypt!"

She screamed in excitement making the other people on the line look to see what was happening. Calvert continued, "That's why your Mom was going through your things. She was packing for you."

"You mean she knows about this?"

"Of course she does...I had to ask your father's permission to take you away, didn't I? In fact she came with me to check in earlier."

Beth shook her head in disbelief.

"What? We've always wanted to go to Egypt! And now to visit an actual excavation site??? This is..."

"I love you!" she jumped on him catching him off guard and almost making him lose his balance.

Over five thousand miles away from home, with the famous pyramids barely visible on the distant sandy horizon, Beth and Cal, dressed in light cotton to withstand the heat, stood at the edge of an active excavation site.

As she watched the workers, Cal let out a shout of excitement behind her. She turned to see him brushing at some sand nearby.

"I think I've found something." he said eagerly and she came over to take a look. Indeed, there seemed to be something in the sand. As she knelt down to take a closer look, he stood up to watch her. She brushed the sand aside and found what looked like a little wooden box.

"Should we call Xavier to come see?"

"Why don't we investigate ourselves?" he said picking up the box against her protests. As she stared at him in shock at his audacity, she could not help noticing how mischievously cute he looked with that smirk on his face.

"We should see what's in it." he said holding it out to her. "I think you should open it."

She looked at him for a second before she grabbed the box out of his hand.

"Ok…I will!"

His smile seemed to get bigger. Brighter now against his skin which had got darker with its exposure to the sun these past three days.

She fiddled with the latch on the box and opened it. Within the box, cushioned in red velvet, lay a ring! She opened her mouth to speak, but nothing came out.

Looking up from the ring, she found Cal on his knees. *Could his smile get any bigger?* she wondered.

"Bethany Clarice Barnes…" he began. Already the tears were welling up in her eyes. "…will you make me the happiest Pharaoh alive and be my queen?"

She could not bring herself to say anything and in the next moment she burst into uncontrollable convulsive laughter. The Pharaoh began to wonder if she was suffering from dehydration. He rose to his feet and reached out to steady her. She grabbed him violently and pulled him close to kiss his lips, now salty from the sandy desert air,

"Calvert Lambeau III…Yes, I will!"

1

It was a sunny afternoon on Penn Street. All the lawns were neatly kept. Only a few cars could be seen in the driveways as most had been driven to various workplaces. Apart from the leaves rustled by the gentle breeze, the cheerful birds chirping and the occasional dog barking, it was very quiet. This was the kind of peace the Lambeaus had sought when looking for a home. If you got close enough to the house at the corner of Penn and Mortimer, you could hear a humming noise coming from inside.

It was Beth doing the weekly vacuuming of her exceptionally kept living room. She had her weekly schedule planned to the minute and she stuck to it in order to keep her home, family and everything she did in perfect working order. The house was always clean, as were all their clothes. She did laundry twice a week and had the dry cleaning delivered if she did not have the time to pick it up herself. There was a fresh warm meal on the nicely laid table for dinner every night and guests were never turned away. Her glasses sparkled and the dust police would be wasting precious time hoping to find even a speck on her perfectly polished wood furniture.

When Cal came home, she was always there to welcome him with a kiss and she rarely, if ever, refused his sexual advances. She was the perfect wife and mother and was proud of it.

She paused as she often did in front of the fireplace to adjust the pictures that stood and hung above it. The wedding portrait of the smiling newlywed Lambeaus hung in the center of the wall above the mantle overlooking the large comfortable living area. A hand-carved coffee table from Australia centered the room and was surrounded by a variety of comfort seats. Beth and Cal had agreed on this eclectic style of decorating. They did not want to be tied to matching fabrics, colors and styles, but wanted to be open and able to add to their home as the mood inspired them. In this way, they had acquired different styles of furniture from their travels, from other family members, from antique stores and from flea markets, making for a very museum-esque yet cozy feeling. It had been a long time since they'd added anything other than a few small knick-knacks brought home from some out of town business trip or other. Their home, very much like their marriage, had settled.

It was the same.

Always the same.

Just needing upkeep.

Cleaning, dusting, vacuuming.

She looked up at the smiling couple and examined their faces. Their eyes were so young and full of expectations of the excitement, adventure and never-ending love of married life.

Beth sighed and asked the couple "Where have you gone?"

It had been almost twenty years since that day.

The wedding date had been just a little rushed after they discovered that Beth had become pregnant in Egypt. It was a dream come true and they had never felt more in love. They did not go on a honeymoon; choosing instead to set up a home in a cozy apartment close to her family and conveniently near to the college where Calvert was working on his Masters in Political Science.

Cal, ever the gentleman, became even more of one when it was determined that they were having a girl. He was beside himself with pride and joy. Nefertiti, he called her, honoring the country where she had been conceived. He walked on air. The pregnancy had been a joyful, easy and healthy time for Beth until she gave birth at thirty-two weeks.

Little Nefertiti weighed just under four pounds and was seventeen and a half inches long. She had a tuft of thick black hair right on the top of her head and the longest eyelashes Beth had ever seen on a baby. She had ten beautiful little fingers and toes. She was in every way perfect, except, she was still.

The doctors tried hard to explain that the umbilical cord had failed to attach to the placenta properly causing a blood vessel to rupture, but none of their medical jargon could explain away the loss of this precious life that had only hours before given a strong and healthy heart beat at her weekly checkup. It was impossible to explain the intense pain that came with the fact that they would be taking Nefertiti home in a box, and not the car seat that Cal had so carefully mounted in the back seat of their car.

Beth cried inconsolably for weeks on end. The sight and sound of anything related to babies, even the litter of stray kittens from across the street, sent her into a downward spiral of gloom.

The cloud that Cal had been walking on became dark and stormy and eventually burst forth a torrent of tears which he tried to hide from her as he locked himself in the bathroom. He needn't have bothered, she was too engrossed in her own pain to feel or even care about his.

Her mother came by every day to cook and clean and fuss over them both. Her father, in his African way, paid his condolences, said a prayer and was done with it. Cal's parents stopped by often to dote on their son. They tried to console her, but she would not let them.

After three years of dating and five months of marriage, this event changed everything about their relationship. They learned to get through grief together, learned to put one foot in front of the other to get by, to seek consolation in Faith, and in God's word, to appreciate each other's silences, and to delight when at last the smiles began to reappear.

But things were changed forever. Even though they had grown closer, they had grown apart.

Marriage and natural physical needs brought them back into each other's arms and they rediscovered each other sexually.

Too soon for the doctors' liking, Beth found herself with child again. This was a much riskier pregnancy and the doctors watched her very closely. At thirty weeks she was aroused out of sleep in severe pain. Cal rushed her to the hospital, both of them praying fervently that this was not a repeat. She had preeclampsia. Her blood pressure was too high. She was admitted and spent the rest of her pregnancy on bed rest, afraid, alone and depressed. Her labor was induced and painful. Eventually, a healthy baby boy was born by C-section and rushed away to the pediatric ICU. She did not get to see him until two days after he was born, but when she did, she was in love. "My miracle baby" she whispered repeatedly as she held him closely for the first time. She burst into tears and as her sobbing worsened, a worried nurse came and saved the little newborn from her. She suffered with postpartum depression even though the child was her pride and joy and her one reason for living.

Cal named the baby Winston, comparing the little one's tenacity to that of British Prime Minister Winston Churchill convincing the United States to become an ally in the Second World War Cal was a proud dad, but he did not have a clue of what to do with or about Beth's moodiness.

It took almost two years for things to finally begin to feel more normal. They fell into their role as a family and began to live like one. She never went back to work. He went on to get his Doctorate and later a Professorship. Pregnancy never again reared its head and she was fine with that. She had come to terms with the fact that she and pregnancy did not get along. So even though she did nothing to prevent it, she was well satisfied that nothing ever developed.

Winston was enough for her and she poured all she had into him.

She touched his photo on the mantel, stroking his cheek. It was a new photo, his high school graduation. Her miracle baby would be leaving for college soon. A grown man. She smiled. There would be a different energy in the home without him there. She looked back up at her smiling husband in the wedding portrait, took a deep breath and turned her vacuum cleaner back on. He'd be home soon and she still needed to change the sheets.

2

As she lay beneath him, her mind raced between thoughts. It took some time before her body got the message that there was something happening. Slowly, at the end of a fleeting reminder that she had to pick up flowers for the Women's Fellowship Gala, her body began to release and get into the rhythmic flow of lovemaking. Then, just as she was matched to his rhythm, he pushed hard and let out a stern growl.

Her first thought was *"That's kind of a turn off when you think about it."* Then, as he shuddered to a stop, her second thought was *"Oh, it's over… but I'm not done yet…"* Her brain sent the message to her body that it should "Cease fire" and this was followed by her third thought, *"Well… better go get ready!"*

He rolled off her apparently satisfied and she jumped out of bed.

"Where are you going now?"

"Got to put on the mac and cheese for Church." She spoke aloud another thought.

"Uh-huh" he mumbled and turned over unenthused.

A while later, as she was putting the macaroni into the oven, he walked into the kitchen noticeably annoyed. He pulled open the fridge door as though he wanted to rip it off its hinges.

"You know, it would really be nice if you didn't always have to run off somewhere to do something for someone else"

He poured himself a glass of orange juice and gulped it down staring at her angrily.

"What are you talking about, Cal?" She asked, genuinely confused.

"Well, what's wrong with spending a little time with your husband, huh? Gotta jump out of bed before we even have a chance to say 'mmm, that was good, care for seconds?'"

"Or maybe finish the first course?" she threw in slyly and saw that she had hit a nerve as his eyes turned stern and cold.

"You think I don't know that you didn't come? But when was I supposed to offer more when you *have* to run off to cook...for *Church*!!!! Oh, so important!!!"

"Cal, you know I need to bring mac and cheese for after service lunch. I always do!"

"Yes, Yes, because there's no one else in that whole church that could bring some Goddamn mac and cheese! All those young girls and their mamas and grand mamas, but it *has* to be you!"

"Well, I volunteered! I want to help out..."

"Well, you could volunteer to me every now and then, you know!"

"Cal, you know, you are being totally ridiculous right now!"

He slammed his glass into the sink, picked up his jacket and began to storm out. At the door he stopped.

"I get it! I am only the side attraction in your life, or maybe I am just the one you are putting up with. I'd really like to spend some quality time with my wife instead of rushing through everything we do because she's got to run off to save anybody else that might need saving. Just anything to be away from me. . . ."

"What? But Cal, everything I do is for you"

"Well, then fucking stop doing shit *for* me and do something *with* me for a change!!! 'Cause hey, if you don't want to be here, why the hell are you?"

He slammed the door, leaving her staring after him in total shock.

♉

A well packaged aluminum foil tray of mac and cheese stood on the granite kitchen counter.

Beth, her clothes neatly laid out on the bed, stared at her reflection in the bathroom mirror as she got ready for church. She brushed her hair into an obedient ponytail and noticed that her hands were shaking. She cursed out loud, angry at herself that she let him get to her in this way.

This was not the first time they'd argued about her so-called 'non-essential' obligations. It was also not the only argument they'd had in the last week. Arguments had become quite the norm in the last few months. But this was the first time he had said anything like that. *"...if you don't want to be here, why the hell are you?"* She replayed the words in her mind. Was he seriously implying that she did not *want* to be here?

Tears welled up in her eyes. She truly meant it when she said that everything she did was for him. The church was *his* church. Those mamas and grandmamas he spoke about were women that *he* grew up with, who had watched him grow in the hope that he would marry one of their own daughters one day. She had become active in church to become better acquainted with his church friends, to make sure they knew that he had done good and married a good woman and to give her son a spiritual home that both parents belonged to. The congregation welcomed her, but she could sense the suspicion and distrust among the women so she made every effort to fit in and be accepted.

Other 'non-essentials' included babysitting *his* nieces while his sister worked two jobs, being an ever present mother to their son, being an active PTA member and parent coordinator at his various schools *and* helping out at the University whenever it was called for.

Appearances were important and it was needful that she always present herself as an intelligent and well-rounded wife to her rising star professor husband.

It all did not make sense! He was mistaken and she would not let this affect her time in church today.

She took a deep breath, lifted her chest and decided that everything was alright, and that this was the front she would show in church.

And so she did.

No one said anything, or asked why they did not sit together, it seemed that no one knew anything was awry, and she was not going to be the one to let on. They both smiled and went through all the motions of a regular Sunday service.

At lunch, she thought how much she hated the *'God-damn'* mac and cheese as she placed it at the center of the lunch table, ready to be served.

"Sister Beth, could you please help to serve today? I am just not feeling up to it." Sister Toni said standing beside her. As she looked up to respond, she could see Calvert shaking hands with a few of the brothers as he made his way out. She felt a sharp pain go through her chest, but composed herself enough to reply,

"Er. . . Yes, yes, of course, no problem!"

She had been home a long while before he came in. He held up the two bags he was carrying and smiled.

"Your favorites!" he said coming towards her at the dishwasher she was in the process of emptying. "Tandoori Chicken, Samosas, Naan and Mango Lassi"

"That's nice. Thanks." she said blandly and turned to place a dish back into a cabinet.

He came up behind her and put his arms around her waist.

She prayed that he could not feel her anger rise and her body stiffen. He probably could, but didn't seem to care.

He kissed her neck.

"Beth! I'm sorry. I know I hurt your feelings with the things I said this morning and I am truly sorry. I guess I was angry but that's no excuse. I want you to know that I appreciate you and every little thing you do. It makes you you. And I love you."

He turned her to face him and she prayed that he would not feel her anger subside and her body soften. He probably could, but didn't seem to care.

He waited to hear her response.

Damn this man, she thought raising her white flag in surrender, *how does he always know just what to say?* She looked up at him. He was searching her eyes.

"I'm sorry." he repeated softly.

"I…um…I…" she stammered and before an entire word could be formed, her surrender was complete. Her arms were around his neck, their lips were hungrily entwined, his hands were moving fast and furiously to undress her.

They made love. The making up kind. The passionate, making up kind. It moved from the kitchen to the stairs, to the bedroom. It was like young love. It was uninhibited. Free. Good.

He came out of the shower just as she was getting dressed and announced,

"Let's go to Marla's party!"

"Excuse me? What party?"

"The Department party at Marla's house."

"You didn't tell me there was going to be a party."

"Well, I didn't think I was going to want to go…but now I do."

"What's this about?"

With sarcastic charm he reported, "Our hot shot professor, Marla Miralta's most recent publication has received mention in the Wall Street Journal based on which she has been invited to be an 'expert' on Lou Dobbs next week."

"Oh, that's cool! I am surprised you didn't want to go. I think we should. Besides, we need to start finding other things to do now that Winston is leaving us, eh?"

"I could think of a thing or two." He winked.

They both laughed and got dressed for the party.

3

The party was abuzz with the regular academic conversation. It was a lot bigger than Cal had made out.

Everyone who was anyone in the Faculty was there, as well as some of the new PhD. students and some of Marla's favorite top undergraduates. The dining table was decked to the max with hors d'oeuvres of every kind and the kitchen counter served as a bar, complete with shot glasses, sliced lime and salt to accompany the Patron Tequila.

Marla had welcomed them with enthusiasm at the door, giving Beth a warm embrace presumably to make up for the long time since they'd last seen each other.

"Cal, this is wonderful!" she had yelled in her strong Argentine accent. "Thanks so much for coming. I have just the drink for you two. Come!" She led the way to the kitchen and poured them each a frozen cocktail from the blender.

"It is sweet and strong." She smiled. "Just the way to get the night started! Enjoy!"

And with that she had sauntered off leaving Beth staring after her perfectly sculpted rear rolling away into the crowd.

"Ugh!" said Cal. "It really is sweet! You like it?"

She took a sip of hers, "Mmm, yes, I do."

"Well then you can have mine. I'll set it in the fridge while you get through the first one. I'm keeping this simple...a beer for me." He helped himself to one, gave her a kiss on the cheek and launched into his party networking mode moving effortlessly between the people who mattered.

She'd got through her frozen drink and it had produced the necessary effect. She was relaxed, lively, maybe a little tipsy, and she had become a part of the party buzz. After a pleasant chat with the Dean and his wife, she figured it was time to get that refill from the fridge.

Cal was nowhere in sight.

She headed to the kitchen.

With the new glass in her hand, she scanned the party from the kitchen entrance, deciding how to spend the next segment of time and with whom. Joining Cal's conversation might be nice, if only she could find him. *Perhaps he is on the balcony*, she thought and decided that some fresh air would do her good anyway.

She made her way back out into the living room.

As she passed by the dining table she could not resist the little cream puffs. She placed two carefully on a small dessert plate, prepared to move on and then gave into the temptation of having just one more. She placed the third puff gently on to her plate, covertly checking if anyone was watching. Satisfied, she turned on her heel to leave. But the high heel of her shoe had got caught in the rug when she turned so as she attempted to step away, her foot would not move. Already leaning forward to make the next step, she lost her balance. Frantically she tried to save the plate, the drink and herself, but gravity got the better of all three. She fell against the table which seemed to give under her weight. Her reflex was to drop the glass and reach forward to break the fall that was sure to come. The glass shattered on the floor and the sweet cocktail splattered on her and everywhere else, but there wasn't time enough to focus on that as she found herself heading in the same direction. She fell with one arm crushing the cream puffs and the other arm crushing the broken glass, her knees hitting the ground awkwardly behind her.

The loud crash caused the conversation to stop and everyone turned their focus in her direction.

"I'm okay!" she lied, grossly embarrassed and feeling the pain in her knees and arms. And then, as if it were a grand finale to the show, she heard the 'pop' and knew that she could not move because if she did, her dress would literally fall off her. The zipper had burst.

"Ground, please swallow me up." she murmured quietly as she cursed herself for not having worn her girdle. What on earth was she thinking?

Everything seemed to be happening in slow motion, and all the voices sounded slurred in her head. After what felt like painful hours, Cal was hovering over her. She recognized his shoes, and looking up, she saw his hand in front of her.

"What the hell, Beth…are you alright? Are you hurt? What happened?" he was saying.

She grabbed his hand for support as she tried to pull herself up while holding her dress closed in an attempt to hide the love-handles she was sure were on display.

"Are you okay?" His voice was gentle and caring, but looking up at him, she saw that his eyes belied his voice and words. He quickly looked away, seemingly focusing on keeping her covered as he pulled her up, but she had caught it and she was quite certain that what she saw in his eyes was contempt and even disgust.

Suddenly Marla's loud Spanish cursing from behind the guests brought Beth back into real time. "*Correte*, get out of my way, can't you see she is hurt!" she was yelling as she approached with a blanket and literally pushed Cal out of the way. Beth was standing now, albeit very unsteadily. Her left arm was covered in vanilla cream, her right in blood, and her dress in both. Marla threw the blanket around her and supporting her, led her away into her bedroom. Cal remained looking after them and though Beth thought of looking back at him, she wasn't sure she wanted to.

"*Mi amor*, are you alright?"

"Yes, yes, I am fine." Beth pretended. She felt herself fighting the intense feelings that were rising within her. She had to keep a straight face, she told herself. If only she could get away from Marla and have a solitary moment.

But Marla was going nowhere. She brought a wet flannel from the bathroom and methodically began to clean Beth's arms. Discovering the source of the blood from several cuts on Beth's right hand and arm, she cursed under her breath and went back to the bathroom for her first aid kit.

Beth just stared, saying nothing.

Marla smiled at her as she bandaged one of the cuts.

"You do know that there are better ways to command a man's attention, don't you?"

"A man's attention?...no...I ...I just tripped. I am just a klutz...I lost my balance and I...."

"I am just joking *querida*, you seemed to be so far away...I was just trying to bring you back."

"Oh" Beth blushed. "Yes, you are right...I'm sorry...I was somewhere else...thank you so much for this."

Marla smiled and took away the first aid equipment. When she returned, she began rummaging through her closet. "Now, let's see..."

Beth watched her as she moved around casually. Marla was the kind of woman you needed to envy. She was a self-made success story, having immigrated from Argentina on her own at a young age. With resolute ambition, she had worked her way to the top. Now here she was, about to become a television personality. Beth guessed her to be in her fifties. She was beautiful, smart, respected and well liked. She had an awesome body that looked great in clothes and had thick black hair that glistened with slight streaks of gray. Not to mention the thick sexy Argentinian accent. There was nothing ordinary about her, she was everything Beth was not.

"...let's get you out of that dress and into something else." Marla was saying.

Beth let out a sarcastic sneer.

"Yeah right, and now you are making fun of me? What are you...a size 8? And I am a 14...you couldn't possibly have anything other than a bath robe in that closet that I could fit into. But hey, that's okay...I can wear it and sneak out the back...or why hide? Maybe I could party on in my robe."

"First of all...I am proud to be a voluptuous size twelve. I may look slimmer because of my height but I have no respect for the single digits. A woman should look well fed. And secondly, as it happens, I *do* have something that you can wear." She pulled out a maroon slightly fitted flowing dress. It had a low cleavage and high slits on the sides.

"Oh, Marla, I couldn't wear that!"

"*Por que no?* I am pretty sure it will fit."

"Yes, but...well...it's kind of...well...I'm just a little more conservative than that."

"It's sexy?"

"Yup, that's it."

"And you are not sexy?"

"Not like *that*."

"You don't think this is better than the bathrobe?"

"Very funny! I just don't usually wear those kinds of dresses."

"Well, I think you should. It would look good. I am sure your husband would not mind too, eh? Wink, wink!"

Beth could no longer conceal her emotions and burst into tears taking Marla completely by surprise.

"*Bueno, esta bien* Beth, you don't have to wear the dress."

"It's okay...I will wear it. Who cares anyway?"

Marla was speechless.

"I don't know what I've done," Beth continued, "but I can't seem to right it. He hates me, I know he does."

"What are you talking about, Beth?"

"Cal! He hates me. He doesn't love me anymore...and I just don't know what I am supposed to do with myself."

Marla finally moved from where she was standing and came towards her.

"Goodness Beth…you could not be more wrong. Trust me, I work with the man…he loves you dearly. He talks about you all the time."

"You only work with him. You don't *know* him."

"Well…maybe, but I cannot imagine that he would not love you Beth…what is not to love?"

Beth cried, leaving Marla at a loss again.

"I'm sorry…I'm sorry I messed up the party, broke your glass and all that…I'm sorry I am here…I'm…"

"Stop it, Beth!" Marla's tone had completely changed. She sounded stern. *Probably the way she sounds to her students,* Beth caught herself thinking. She grabbed Beth by the shoulders and shook her gently.

"You stop this right now! *Entiendes?* Do not apologize for being yourself EVER!! You hear me? You look for your worth inside and you own it! Don't let your husband define you! You are a beautiful intelligent woman…I shouldn't have to tell you this…act like you know it! *Escuchas?* You don't have to apologize for a mess…that is what happens at parties, people have a good time, people make a mess…so what? But you know what *is* a mess? Your face right now…your make up is everywhere. So, you are going to freshen up, put on this dress and come outside and have a good time, ok? YOU…have a good time! Ok?"

Beth nodded.

Marla took a deep breath and got up to leave, "*Bueno!* There are towels in the bathroom and you may help yourself to any of the make up on the dresser if you need it…see you soon."

She smiled and was gone.

Solitude! Finally!

But Marla had not left her with the self-pitying emotions she had wanted to indulge in. She had challenged her. And now Beth was deciding whether to take the challenge or not. She looked in the mirror and saw that Marla was right…she *was* a mess. Well, challenge or not…she could not go out looking like that, so she might as well get cleaned up.

She looked around the room. It had a very feminine feel to it. Beth thought it actually felt somewhat erotic. She chuckled to herself. *Everything about this woman is sexy.*

Sexy!

She looked at the dress laid out on the bed for her.

Sexy!

She did wear sexy lingerie in the bedroom at times. And in times gone by, she and Cal did play some "sexy" games, but for the most part she shied away from overly suggestive clothing.

She ventured into the bathroom. It was just like the bedroom - feminine, inviting, sultry. The bathtub had candle votives standing by and there was a lit scented candle on the window sill giving the room a deliciously sweet smell of Jasmine. Beth let her imagination run a little wild, picturing herself making love in this beautiful bathroom with Cal. Cal! *I just can't help myself, can I?* she scolded herself as she headed to the sink to wash up.

Back in the bedroom, she sat at the dresser in front of the mirror and examined the array of make-up, perfumes and jewelry Marla had out. There was a red embroidered box standing behind the perfumes. *Hmm, wonder what kind of perfume that is,* Beth thought as she reached for it. Opening it, she blushed finding that it contained not a bottle of perfume, but a stash of condoms. "Oops…definitely sexy! And that'll teach you to stop being nosy" she said out loud to herself.

Some time later, she stood fully dressed in front of the full length mirror that hung on the back of the bedroom door. Marla had been right, the dress did fit her. Her cleavage looked tempting, and the rest of the dress clung to her just enough to look curvy without being offensive. The slits on the side could not be seen unless she moved and then they opened up all the way to her mid-thigh. *On Marla those slits must ride up to her hips* Beth thought as she examined herself.

There was a knock at the door and Marla peeked in.

"Are you alright? We are beginning to get worried…Hey! Look at you!…*Divina!* You need to get out here…there is a handsome man waiting."

Beth smiled, picked up her clutch and walked out of the bedroom passing by Marla.

Cal was right at the door waiting for her.

He had been looking concerned, but when he saw her, his eyes widened. He looked her up and down and smiled,

"Wow, was your Fairy God Mother in there or something?"

"You could say that" Beth smiled and winked at Marla.

"Well you look divine" he said as he pulled her close and gave her a reassuring hug. "I love you."

The next morning, Beth sat drinking a cup of tea as she stared at Marla's dress hanging in front of her, ready to be returned.

Amazing what a dress can do, she mused as she replayed the rest of the night over in her head again.

It had been pleasant enough until the drive home, when she brought up the accident. He seemed less than supportive telling her that maybe she could benefit from some time at the gym.

"What are you saying?"

"Well, if you find yourself bursting out of your clothes, seems to me that you got too big for them. So you can buy bigger clothes, or lose some weight. Simple enough! I mean it is kind of embarrassing, isn't it?"

"Did I embarrass you?"

"Didn't *you* feel embarrassed?"

"So do you find me disgusting?" she dared to ask.

"Well, not in that dress right there…far from it" he giggled.

She was not getting where she wanted with this conversation, so she ended it, turning to look out the window. "Whatever!"

But sitting here now, she remembered that look she'd seen in his eyes again. Whatever was he thinking at that moment? He couldn't possibly dislike her that much or he would not be able to turn one hundred and eighty degrees just because she was wearing a sexy dress, or could he?

Maybe all their relationship needed was a little more spice? A little more daring in their sex life. He did say he'd want to spend more 'quality' time with her and sex was always a big part of 'quality' for him. She smiled. "Whatever!" she said to herself pouring out her unfinished tea and just as she did so, she had a brain wave. *No time like the present!* She would kill two birds with one stone. When returning the dress to Marla's office on campus, she would stop by his office and bring a picnic basket of lunch. She would wear something cute and cheeky and if he had the time, they could have a picnic right there at work. And who knows where that could lead.

Brilliant!

After fixing the lunch basket, complete with a picnic sheet to sit and hopefully cuddle up on, she ran up the stairs and pulled out a cute turquoise summer dress. Its floral bustier was held up by spaghetti straps and below it, smooth pleats opened up right above the waist lending to a flowing skirt which was very complimentary to her stomach and hips. A pair of matching strappy one inch heels completed her 'casual' look. She smiled at herself, blew herself a kiss and ran back down, stuffing Marla's dress and a thank you card into her tote bag. She'd drop those off first.

On campus, she was somewhat relieved that Marla was not in her office. She still felt a little embarrassed about her melt down last night. She got a large envelope from the department general office, put the dress and the card into it and left it in Marla's mail cubby.

Then she sprayed some Strawberries'n'Cream Victoria's Secret body spray over herself and bounced excitedly down the stairs heading for Cal's office.

Approaching his door, she stopped, adjusted her dress and hair, held the basket in front of her and proceeded.

His door was only slightly ajar. She knew that he always left his door wide open when he had visitors to avoid any possible suggestion of inappropriate behavior and the like, so she thought he must either be alone, or have stepped out. As she planned how best to stage her surprise, she heard voices from inside. She would not be able to barge in with a picnic basket if he was having a meeting so she stepped a little closer to take a peek into the room.

Even though the woman was backing her, Beth recognized her instantly.

You could not mistake that glorious head of hair which right now was being thrown back in laughter.

No problem with laughter, but there was definitely a problem with Cal's arms around her waist, and an even bigger problem with the way he was looking at her.

Beth recognized that look, it was the same aroused look he had when he looked at her last night at the party when she'd stepped out in that dress. Marla's dress.

4

It was not stealth vigilance that kept Beth silently watching.

It was more like paralysis.

"You keep your hands to yourself, Prof. Lambeau," Marla laughed, "the party is one thing, the office is quite another, we have an agreement about this"

Cal watched her every move as if mesmerized, the lust in his eyes unmistakable.

Some noise down the hall as a group of students barged in woke Beth from her paralysis and shook the lovers apart. Cal seemed to be heading toward the door. Beth took off, running down the hall and out of the building as fast as the one inch heel sandals could carry her. She threw the basket into the car, jumped in herself and began to drive well above the speed limit to get just as far away as she could, as quickly as she could.

She was incapable of logical thought.

She was incapable of mature rational reasoning.

She was raw emotion.

She pulled into a gravel drive way, hit the brakes and came to a sharp stop. And then she sat, staring at the steering wheel, slowly calming down. Shock, anger, disappointment and hurt all pulled at her for preeminence. She began to be aware of herself again. She was sweating, breathing fast, hands shaking. She looked up through the wind shield and realized that raw emotion had brought her home to Mama. She was at her parents' home.

She laughed at the realization that her inner child had taken over. The problem was she was not a child. She was a grown woman, a married woman, married to a cheat…..and Mama would not be able to kiss this booboo better.

Yet here she was.

She got out of the car and as she closed the door, she caught sight of the picnic basket in the back seat. Suddenly anger won over all the other emotions. She ripped open the back door yanking the basket out with a growl and launched a fierce attack on it; ripping and flinging its contents around the driveway, throwing the basket to the ground and kicking it with all the force of a bad cop.

"What *is* going on here? Bethany, what *are* you doing? Look at you!"

"Mom!" Beth looked up from her victim and saw her mother standing before her. She had just walked in the driveway dressed in sweats as though she had been jogging.

For a second they just stared at each other. The mother, knowing something was very wrong. The daughter, catching her breath and not knowing where to start.

"You want to come in the house?"

"Mom…" deep breathing, "Mom…" head shaking, "Mom…." anger leaving, sadness flooding in, "Oh, Mom…" flood gates opened and she was in her mother's embrace.

"…..so he finally did it. He finally found himself a cheerleader"

Beth sat at the kitchen counter while her mother moved around preparing dinner.

"Oh please Beth, you are his biggest cheerleader of all. Have been all these years. He knows that."

"Yeah, but I don't look like a cheerleader, Mom"

"Well, if looks is all it's about…"

"Then what, Mom? Then it's ok?"

"Now, I didn't say that"

"What *do* you say, Mom? You have been awfully quiet since I mentioned it. One could almost think you were on his side. I know you adore Cal, so maybe you are."

"It's not about choosing sides, Beth"

"So why don't you just tell me what is going on in your head, Mom. What are you thinking about all this?"

"Honey, whatever *I* say has nothing to do with *your* situation right now. You are hurt and you need to work through that first."

"Damn right, I'm hurt!!! And I was hoping for comfort from my mother I guess. So why don't you just give me that instead of this calm therapist type thing you're putting on?"

"And how much good would it do if I got all worked up like you right now? You have to work through the hurt and get back to your peace so you can think straight"

"I am not asking for Oprah's answer, Mom! I am asking for sympathy! For compassion! Feel with me!"

Her mother dropped the tomatoes she was about to chop up and came round the counter to give her daughter a hug.

"Oh Beth, I do feel with you. You know I've been there. I know this place all too well and I am so sorry that you have to be there too. And that is why I know that it would not be wise for me to jump right in and feed into your anger. To what end? This is *your* marriage. *You* have to work through it. Trust me on this."

Beth pushed her away giving her an incredulous stare.

"You don't really think I am going to 'work through this', do you? Mom, I am so not you. I am not going to be any man's door mat…not even Professor Calvert Fucking Lambeau the Third. No way!"

"You may call me a door mat Beth, but I made my choices and I have stood by them. Now you must make yours. All I ask is that you don't make them in anger. And I will stand by you whatever you choose."

"Yes Mom, you did make your choices...again and again. Why would you do that? Well, you are a better woman than me, because one chance is all Cal is getting. This is not going to happen again."

"It was a different time back then, I was a white girl married to an African...my family was none too impressed...I'd given up my life as I knew it for this man...where was I going to go?"

"He knew you'd always be there when he got home from screwing those whores and he took full advantage of it. I couldn't believe that you would even share your bed with him knowing fully well where he'd been."

"Beth...check yourself! Before you get really disrespectful. Now, I know you are angry but like I said before, this is *your* marriage. You leave me and your father out of it, okay? How easy it would be to leave, right? It would solve everything, right? But does it really? Does it solve the underlying undiscussed problems? Look, I have lived my life and I lived it the way I wanted. And now I am at a place in my life where everything is in balance. Yes, it took a lot of hurt and hard work to get here, but I am here! And I love it here! I love *me* here! So you can judge me all you want but if you want to get to where I am, you need to get over yourself. Nobody is perfect you know, not Cal and not you either. Sometimes men do these things. Sometimes they need to. Sometimes you need to let them. But you shouldn't focus on him... focus on you! Sometimes it works out...sometimes not."

Beth shook her head in disbelief,

"...let him???" she repeated.

She began to pace, weighing her anger at Cal against the anger that was building against her mother right now.

"I better go!" She stated the best solution, "I can't talk to you right now. Does Dad still have The Farm?"

Her mother nodded.

"Could I have the keys? I need to hang out there for a while."

"Oh honey, the place is a mess. We haven't been out there in ages. It's probably over grown with shrubbery and weeds"

"Mom... the keys?"

"They are in the key dish in the living room"

Beth rushed to the other room for the keys and came flying through the kitchen heading for the door.

"And don't you *dare* tell Cal where to find me"

"Why?...How long will you stay? Can I tell your father? And what about your son?"

"They are grown men, Mom, I'm sure they'll be fine! Well, ok... you can tell Stoney if you need to...and I don't care what you tell Dad."

Without another look back at her mother, she hurried out.

Nothing calms quite like a hot shower.

The warm water mixed with her warm tears, running down her face and neck, flowing over and around her breasts and down across the curves of her body which she compared to Marla's curves of perfection as she looked down at herself.

She stepped out of the water stream, grabbed the loofah and began to scrub viciously, from her hair down to her toes, as though she could rub off all that was herself. But at the end, no longer crying or angry and covered with sweet smelling lather, she found that she was still she.

She stepped back under the water and stood still, letting the water wash off the lather on its own. Her skin, sore from scrubbing, seared under the warm water but it felt good. She felt strangely calm. Even content. Or maybe it was denial. Whatever it was, it offered a welcome reprieve from the earlier turmoil.

Nevertheless, calm as she seemed, she avoided the mirror when leaving the bathroom and getting dressed.

Feeling invigorated, she began to pack a large duffel bag. She still thought it a good idea to get away for a while. Think things through. Make sense of it. Maybe her mother was right about not taking action in anger. A couple of days away should do her some good….*and would make him realize what he'd miss,* her inner self sneered…but almost immediately another part of herself countered, *or would it?*

Insecurity mounting, she realized she had to get out of the house before he got home. She could not bear the idea of him looking at her like some second rate woman. The loser. The failure.

She hurried and got everything into the car but just as she was turning off the lights and getting ready to leave, he walked in.

He smiled at her, oblivious. "Hey"

Her heart was in her throat but still she felt calm. "Hey!" she responded.

He moved around like normal, dropping his keys, hanging up his jacket, starting to take off his shoes, looking up at her puzzled every now and then. Probably wondering why she was standing there frozen, just watching him.

"What's up?" he finally asked.

Something inside her spoke, "How long?"

"Huh?"

She let the thing inside her speak again, "How long Cal, have you been seeing your Argentine Professor?"

Shock streaked across his face, followed by fear. She could see that he knew he had been busted.

He ran toward her with his arms outstretched, but she avoided him.

"Please don't touch me. Just tell me how long."

Beth did not recognize this bold woman who stood staring him straight in the eyes knowing she did not want to hear what he had to say, but she let her lead.

He held her gaze for a moment and then looked away and replied, "A few months"

"Months???" The strange woman laughed an unrecognizable laugh, "God, I am even more naïve than I thought"

"…but babe, it doesn't mean anything…"

"Oh, of course it doesn't…for a few months…and it means nothing…I understand…it's just physical, just sex, it's not emotional, right?"

"Well, it's *not* emotional!"

"Why, Cal? Why did you do it? Have I ever said no to you? Have I ever been anything other than a dutiful wife? Why? Why did you do it?"

"I didn't mean to, Beth…it just…it just happened in a moment of weakness."

"A moment? A few *months* of moments of weakness! That's a lot of weakness for you, Professor"

"Beth, she was there for me when I needed someone"

"And where was I?"

"Well…you were…the reason I needed someone"

"Excuse me?"

"Oh, don't let's pretend like everything's been rosy. We had a row, you were pissed, I needed to talk, she listened."

"Uh hun"

"…but then she did more than listen"

"Well, we all know that!"

"No, I mean she would help me see your side, and she would tell me what to say and do to win you over, and it always worked. She was always right. She was helping us make it better"

"Are you listening to yourself?" Beth was back in form. Pure anger.

"But isn't it true, though? Haven't we been getting better?"

"No, Cal!…We have not been getting better. We are unhappy, we argue and fight and YOU ARE SLEEPING WITH ANOTHER WOMAN!!!"

"Beth, I really only wanted you back the way it used to be"

"Well, you did a damn good job of it because I am leaving." She targeted the door.

"No Beth, please don't. We can work this out. Let's talk this through. Don't just leave like that. I know I made a mistake, but I would take it all back in an instant to keep you from leaving"

"Did she prepare you for this moment too? Gave you the right lines to feed me? Not this time, Honey. And you know what, I may not be as smart as she is, but I have some effective choice words too. Like FUCK YOU!"

"Beth! Stop this! Please!"

She headed out the door and to the car with him at her heels. She revved the engine and let down the window enough so she could show him the middle finger and throw him one last "Fuck you!"

5

Beth was awakened by a loud noise from outside.

She rolled over in bed moaning as she noticed the deep throbbing ache in her head. She sat up and took in her surroundings, confused. Rubbing her temples, it slowly came back to her that she was at The Farm in what used to be her parents' bedroom. The room was very simply furnished with a mission style poster bed, matching armoire and dresser, the latter two of which were still covered with white sheets. Her duffel bag lay open on the floor with some of her things strewn around it. White sheets which she had obviously pulled off the bed lay nearby. She vaguely remembered pulling them off and putting on her own sheets from home. The droning noise outside would not stop. Angrily she headed to the window to investigate, making a huge effort not to succumb to the dizziness that came with her upright position. There was a man mowing the lawn next door.

"This early in the morning?" she mumbled to herself, "How inconsiderate!"

She unlocked the window latch with some difficulty and threw it open, yelling out to the man,

"Hey you…Do you have to do this so early? Some of us are trying to get some sleep here. Cut out the noise"

The man seemed to wave back at her smiling. She wasn't sure.

"Just knock it off!" She yelled and slammed the window shut, "Oooh" she moaned as her head seemed to explode with the slam.

"Coffee…kitchen…sleep…bed…mmm"

She let herself fall back onto the bed and pulled the covers over her head trying to get back to sleep despite the spinning and the pain. This just seemed easier than going down to the kitchen. Surely if she could get back to sleep, she would wake up feeling better.

The noise finally stopped and there was silence. She stayed under the sheets and in the silence her jumbled thoughts began to fall into place like a jigsaw puzzle…a clear image beginning to form.

She had driven the thirty some miles from home drowning out her thoughts with Maroon 5's latest CD playing at full volume and making only two stops. One for gas, and the other for a few essential groceries that she might need at The Farm, including two bottles of Chardonnay, a large box of Ferrero Rocher chocolates, a chocolate frosted marble cake and other less essential edibles and toiletries. She had every intention of drinking herself into a stupor.

She had arrived at dusk and stood outside the gate before letting herself in.

"The Farm!" she had whispered under her breath.

It had been her parents' weekend home when she was young. Among other firm convictions, her father believed in eating of the earth, so he had purchased the land from an elderly lady who had gardened on it passionately until she no longer could. Her only consolation in selling the land was knowing that this little African man was as passionate about growing his own food as she had been. When the Barnes' first bought it, the land had only a little garden shack on it, but over time, they had built it into a home away from home. The original shack now made up the living room, and a full bathroom. To it, they added a kitchen and a large storage space which opened to the outside and over that, they built another floor with two bedrooms and a tiny play/sitting area.

The yard used to be a beautiful canvas of nature's art, covered with shades of green speckled with the bright colors of fruits, vegetables and flowers. A swing hung from the apple tree which stood in the front and provided shade, juice and turnovers all year round.

"The Farm"

She had taken a deep breath and was immediately transported to another time.

She could see herself laughing and joyous as she created adventurous stories that took her all around the yard. She investigated every plant and every creature she came across. She danced freely under the sprinklers. At night she would play board games with her parents or on her own. She wrote, she sang, she danced, she drew. Life was so easy back then. Not to say that she had no responsibilities, her father would not hear of that and she did not mind it because it was their time together. She helped him on the farm, turning the soil, planting, weeding, harvesting. Collecting berries and cucumbers in baskets and snacking on them at the same time. She was usually so full after picking, that she did not have room in her little tummy for dinner. These were the times when she shared laughter with her father. Times when he knew she was there and she knew that he knew it. He would call her name in that sweet African accent, the way he did and would show her how to prune a shrub properly, or how to graft a stem. He would smile at her and hold her close and brag about her when they went indoors. He was always someone else out here.

But she was not the only one who experienced him differently.

Out here, her Mom and Dad seemed to genuinely care for each other. This always seemed doubtful when they were at home in the city. It seemed working the land together always brought them back together. In the city, they seemed to live separate lives. He always came home late and her mother scheduled her life around his absence. Often they would argue about his infidelities which he was none too discreet about. Once, when Beth was a young teen, she watched from her window as her father arrived home in a strange woman's car. He leaned over and kissed the woman on the lips before he stepped out and walked to the house with an extra pep in his step. Beth ran downstairs to warn her mother, but she needn't have bothered, when she got to the kitchen, her parents were already engaged in a violent argument. She slithered back up to her room, locked the door and turned her radio on full blast. That same weekend, her parents seemed at peace and in love as they raked and shoveled dry leaves together.

By this time, Bethany was no longer blind to the contradiction and as she struggled with her own adolescent demons, she no longer found refuge at The Farm. It felt like a lie. She began making excuses to stay in the city and by the time she and Cal were married, this place seemed like a childhood memory.

It was not lost on her that she was never motivated enough to bring Winston here as he was growing up, even though her parents had suggested it many times. They themselves had abandoned The Farm when her father had taken ill some years ago. He had hoped that his only offspring would continue with what he had handed down to her. He had hoped that he would be able to teach his grandson even more than he had taught her. He had dreamed that this land would be nurtured by his seed for years to come and that the land in turn would nurture his seed.

But he was disappointed. Winston knew nothing of the earth and its richness.

And he was hurt. Bethany, his own off shoot, whose hands he himself had introduced to the dirt; whose coming of age he had watched in amazement right alongside the rose bush they had planted together on her tenth birthday; from her beautiful lips came the suggestion to sell the land. He could not. He would not. He would wait. And he would bequeath it to her.

This land would be hers. Eventually.

Only a stump now remained where the apple tree had stood. There was a mess of green, yellow and brown weeds everywhere. Against the dimming sky and the dark expanse of space behind it, the house stood silent and deserted. Her mother had been right, the lack of care and presence was clear.

Yet, strangely, all these years later, as Beth looked around, she felt comfort. She felt home. This was where she would stay, if only for one night, to be able to think things through.

She unlocked the big padlock that hung on the gate and let herself in.

6

Dunham was typical for a tiny township on the outskirts of a big college town. Most of its inhabitants were in some way or other connected to one of the two colleges in town. Team pride ran just as deep for college teams here as it did for national teams. The actual town itself consisted of an All-American Main Street which ran through its center and was flanked on either side by a spread of a few blocks. Urban sprawl had led to settlements, complexes and small communities all along the linking roads and highways and these were amply catered to by giant malls, grocery stores and multiplexes.

Main Street had all the essentials neatly nestled in quaint little buildings that, except for the paint job, looked like they had not changed since the town was established. Some of the stores were actually still owned and operated by the same families that started them generations ago.

Since Beth had arrived at The Farm five days ago, she had come to town every day.

This was a whole new experience for her since, as a child, her family did not often come to the town. They would bring all their necessities with them and would not need to leave The Farm for their entire stay.

On the first day, she drove to town out of habit, since she rarely walked at home.

Her head still aching after she awoke a second time, she realized that the one thing she had not taken into account when she was planning her alcoholic binge was the hang over that was sure to follow. She desperately needed some painkillers, and thus made her way to town for the nearest pharmacy. She sat at the window in the local diner and took the pills with a cup of coffee and then watched the street while she waited for the effect to kick in.

On the second day, she drove into town out of necessity.

She had woken up much more energized and began pulling the sheets off all the furniture and giving the place a thorough cleaning. Then she brought all the dusty sheets to the laundromat for a wash and had lunch at the diner counter while she waited.

On the third day, she walked to town. And that is what she did every day since.

It was a twenty minute leisurely country side stroll from The Farm to the diner on Main Street. She passed well-kept gardens and greens, even a small farm that sold fresh produce with a little old lady sitting out front waving to Beth as she walked by. Then there were the homes at the edge of town and after two blocks she found herself on Main Street.

Beth found the walk through nature beautiful enough, but she was falling in love with Main Street. She ventured into every open store just to look around and experience it. She chatted with some of the locals but most of the time she kept to herself. At the diner she was quickly making friends with the owners and the staff. No surprise, since each day trip either began or ended here.

Today, after the conversation and coffee, she sat in the far corner, pulled her cell phone out of her bag and turned it on. This would be the first time since she left home.

As expected, there were countless messages from Cal, asking where she was, begging her to come home, begging her to call back, and apologizing repeatedly.

There was a message from her son, just checking in and there were a few messages from her mother checking on her.

She dialed her mother's number.

"Mom? It's me"

"Hey Honey, are you ok?

"Yeah, I am fine. You were right about The Farm though…it needs a lot of work. But I have started cleaning the inside."

"Oh…that's nice…er…Honey…he was here. He was crying, Beth. He calls me every day to know if I heard from you. He is so sorry."

"Mom…that is not what I called for"

"I know, I know, and I am not trying to move you or anything… but I do think you two need to talk. I mean, are you going to stay there forever?"

"I might! It's cozy!"

"Beth!"

"Mom?!?!"

"I just…well, I think you should talk…but that's just me. Do what you feel is right."

"Thanks Mom."

"You sound ok."

"I'm fine! It's nice out here and I am enjoying some alone time."

"Are you going to keep your phone off?"

"Sometimes."

"Ok. Well, thanks for letting me know you are ok. I'll just keep you updated on what's happening here. Ok?"

"Ok, thanks Mom! I appreciate it. I really need this time"

"I understand, Honey. You take care of yourself and call me if you need me. I love you"

"I love you too."

She took a sip of her tea and thought about what her mother had said. When she had come out here it was only supposed to be for one night. Now it had been five and she still had not even dedicated time to really thinking about what had brought her out here in the first place, talk less of talking about it. Maybe she really *should* call him.

She picked up the phone again and dialed...

"Hi, Stoney?"

"Hey Mom! Oh my God! Guess what just happened?"

She couldn't help but smile. Her heart warmed and melted and she relaxed in her seat as she took in his voice. If there was one thing she was always certain of, it was her absolute love for this young person.

"What?" she asked. He sounded as excited as he had been when Cal let go of the back of the bicycle and he realized he was actually riding it himself.

"Jaden and I just scored the most amazing gig, man! We are going on tour with The Solar Dee-Jays. Oh my God! I am so psyched! Mom, they interviewed us personally, they are so cool, I just can't believe it..."

He went on, occasionally throwing a comment to his best friend, Jaden. But Beth had left the conversation... "Hold on, young man, you are going to college in September, will the tour be done by then?"

"Well, we're going to have to talk about that, Mom. We are on for nine months, so I can't start school in September. Look, I am not saying I won't do it, I am just postponing it by a year...it could work...it's been done before."

"Stone, you know that college is a priority to your father and I! I hardly think touring with a rock band measures up."

"Ma! They are not a rock band, they are Electronic Dance Music DJs powered solely by Solar energy and promoting the message of environmental consciousness...you would totally be down with them. Grandma would love them...they are like modern day hippies."

"Winston, this is a very serious conversation we are having. Did you tell your father about this?"

"No, this literally *just* happened, right before you called. We met this guy last night and he turned out to be one of their tech guys. So we showed him what we do and he took us in with him today. But you know Mom, we thought we were just getting in to see behind the scenes and stuff, but next thing we are sitting in an office with them and talking programming and art design and then boom 'how would you like to come on tour with us' Whaaaaaa? I am freaking out right now, Ma…I mean how crazy is that???"

Tears welled up in Beth's eyes. Winston was her gem. He had never disappointed her. He had his father's height and intelligence, but did not inherit his sportsmanship, and therefore had a more slender build. His face was a pleasant light mocha fusion of both parents. For some unknown genetic reason his hair had a reddish brown color to it which seemed to bleach out in the sunny summer months and appear darker in the winter. It was probably his parents' one complaint; that he wore his hair in an unkempt afro. He called it his signature. And it complimented his nick name 'Stoney Red'. The name Stone had stuck since as a baby he would call himself Win-'stone' instead of Win-'ston'.

The sciences were his strong point. A self-proclaimed 'geek', he had been creating his own little computer programs since he was in middle school. The older he got, the more elaborate his ideas and programs became. Together with Jaden, he could tinker around for hours creating interactive electronic art designs and the like. They had won every contest in their school and a few others outside. His room did not boast of sports trophies, but of plaques and certificates.

Beth and Cal were well aware of his passion and they were very proud that he was going to be majoring in computer engineering at their Alma Mater in the coming fall. It never occurred to them for a second the Stone would ever step off the path. But now…

"Mom? You there?"

"Yes, yes, I am here…I want to say I am happy for you and I am so proud of you, Stoney, I really am. But I just really don't want you to lose out on college. We'll have to have a talk with Dad about this, ok?

"Mom, Franklin College was established in 1858, I hardly think it's going anywhere in the next one year while this opportunity is a once in a lifetime thing. But fine, I'll call you guys at home tomorrow to talk about it…but I am going to stand my ground on this one, Mom. I am just not going to come home until after the tour, no matter what you say."

At other times she would have scolded him for the impertinence in his response, but there was something else to deal with right now,

"Um…No, let *us* call you…I, er…we may have plans…er…let me know what a good time will be…you can text me, and then we will call you together. And don't call Dad…I want to talk with him about it first, ok?"

She knew this would have to be a conference call. No point bringing a whole other issue into this discussion.

"Yeah, ok. Whatever. Later Mom"

"Ok. Bye now" she heard the click on the other end.

What was happening?

Her world was falling apart around her.

And now, she would have to call him.

She sat at the kitchen table staring at the phone that lay in front of her. The whole way home she had planned and re-planned how this conversation would go. Why on earth was she finding it so hard to call a man that she had been married to for twenty years? It just didn't make sense. She felt guilty that she had not called since she'd left. She felt bad that now she was being forced to call because of something totally unrelated. She felt scared of his reaction. She felt scared of his rejection.

But at the same time she told herself that it was she who had been wronged.

He should be grateful she was calling.

All this thinking and feeling was getting too much. She could sense a headache coming on. Best to get it over with, once and for all. Maybe he would declare his undying love and beg her to come home…but…did she really want to go home yet? Ever? Oh, why was she so confused?

She sighed and dialed her home number. It rang but once…

"So you finally remembered our number?" He sounded worn, his voice more husky than usual.

She was somewhat taken aback since she had only prepared herself for a conversation starting with 'hello?'

"Um…Yeah, Hi, Cal…are you ok?" She felt something like worry sneak in.

"Is that a sincere question, Beth? Because if it is, why the devil are you not here in front of me asking it?"

"…um…you just sound so…tired, I guess"

"Well, I guess *you've* been sleeping well…cos you sound just fine"

She would have to get to the point, "Cal, I know we need to talk, but we have another problem that needs immediate attention"

"Oh, here we go, talking to her husband for the first time after walking out on him and she has '*Another problem that needs immediate attention*'…what else is new??? What was I thinking??? That you might be calling about *me*? Or coming home? Ha! Fool that I am. So what is it, Beth? What else is *so* much more important and immediate than me?"

"Maybe this was not a good idea. Cal, I am not ready for this. I only called because this is about Winston, but perhaps we can't talk yet, maybe…"

"And then she turns to run away the first chance she gets. You know, you always do that! You always chicken away from dealing with difficult situations. You always run away. What? Are you going to hang up now?"

It had crossed her mind, but she did not admit it. She stayed silent.

He calmed down and continued quietly, "We need to talk Beth! We need to see each other. How else are we going to get through this?"

"I feel I need time to think, I need space…don't pressure me"

"We are a couple, Beth. We are supposed to work things through *together*"

"Well, you weren't thinking that when you were banging Professor Argentina, were you?"

Silence. Then,

"Ok, so I deserved that. But I have apologized, and I have ended it. So how much more time and space do you need?"

"Cal, you really think it's that easy? It was a blatant betrayal of trust. You can't just expect me to be all the same as I used to be at the click of a finger."

"Hmph! You haven't been the same as you used to be for a lot longer than the affair you know"

It was definitely time to get to the point;

"Cal, did you know that Winston is planning not to go to college this fall?"

"What?"

"I guess you didn't. Well, he and Jaden have been offered a job on tour with some band for eight months. So he says he's pushing College off for a year."

"Oh wow! That's cool!"

"Cal! Did you hear what I said? That is NOT cool!"

"It would be a great experience for them"

"Are you just trying to piss me off? Do you realize what this means? No college for a whole year or maybe forever! And think of all he will be exposed to…drugs, slutty women, what will become of him?!"

"Ha ha ha…I guess he might find his manhood" Cal laughed.

"Cal! This is serious. We always wanted college for our son."

"Well, he said he'd come back to it. I am sure he will"

"What if he doesn't? What if he gets swallowed up by that crazy world and never comes back to what he was supposed to do? We need to talk him out of it, Cal! I told him we'd call him tonight to talk this through"

"Did you tell him where you'd be calling from?"

"No…I…didn't want to upset him"

"I see!" He took a deep breath. "Well, if you want to talk it through with him, I agree, I think we should. But I don't agree that we should talk him out of it if he really wants to do it. He will only be young once. If he is going to do this sort of thing, now would be the time. Let's find out exactly what it's all about, see if it's legit, see if it sounds like something he could learn from and then we can help him make the best decision, but you have to face it Beth, Stone is just about a grown man now. He needs to be allowed to figure himself out. You can't do that for him. And a year of road experience before settling down to college doesn't sound all that bad to me. Think about it."

"Oh my God! What good are you?" She could feel herself shaking. Angry that she was not being supported.

"Are you hanging up?"

She wasn't about to give him that,

"No!...Ok, fine, let's talk it through with him. I will call you and we can conference him in"

"When are you coming home?"

"I am not!" she declared, ended the call and threw the phone down. "Grrrrr!"

It hadn't gone anything like she had planned or wanted it to.

And neither did the call with Winston that followed.

Cal played along with her charade, not letting on that they were separated at all, but other than that, he was totally on the other side. He was highly impressed by what Winston and Jaden had achieved, especially that they had scored this gig all by themselves. He even gave advice on how they could use their experience to earn extra credits for their college education.

There was nothing she could say that would dissuade Stoney.

At the end of the call, after Stoney had hung up, Cal gently comforted her.

"You were always the primary caretaker, Beth. And you've done an excellent job. You've raised a great kid. I have no doubt that you can trust him. Let him go, Beth." He sounded so gentle, so caring. He knew exactly what she was feeling. She broke down. As far as she could see, she'd lost them both.

7

It was the perfect morning. The sun was up, bright and warm. The sky was blue and clear. The surrounding lawns were luscious and green. Bethany stood in front of her open front door in a bath robe with her arms folded in front of her chest, a hand on her heart.

She focused on a spot in the heavenly infinity and prayed quietly. She asked for strength, wisdom and most of all, peace. She needed peace. Her heart was aching, not proverbially, but physically.

She barely got any sleep the night before. She cried, tossed and turned, hearing Cal's voice over and over and imagining Stoney coming home with arms full of tattoos and needle tracks, trailed by a bunch of groupies who were either pregnant or diseased.

In the early hours of the morning, she made herself a cup of tea and sat in the living room until the sun came up. That's when she came outside.

"What have I done wrong, Lord?" she asked aloud. "What am I supposed to do with myself? What is going to become of me now?"

"Good Morning!" Her reverie was broken by a friendly voice.

She tore her eyes from the blue and tried quickly to focus on the street in front of her. Slowly, he came into view, smiling and waving as he always did.

It was that young kid that had woken her up that first morning when he was mowing the lawn next door. She had seen him almost every day as she walked to or from the town. He was always in someone's yard doing the gardening. It was clear what his passion was. All the yards she'd ever seen him in were immaculate and beautifully kept.

She usually tried to ignore him, but like a typical small town kid, he would still say hello, waving and smiling like he was doing right now. Sometimes, she'd wave back half-heartedly, sometimes she'd just walk on without as much as a glance in his direction. He probably just thought that she was a big city bitch.

True enough I guess, she thought.

She gave him a slight acknowledging nod, turned and walked into the house closing the door firmly behind her. Once inside, she carefully peeked out the window and watched him continue down the street.

"Weirdo!" she said and headed for the shower.

The shower did not perform its magic.

Neither did the bright lime green teeshirt and shorts, she put on.

She felt confused, frustrated, angry and hurt all at once. She had no idea how to best deal with these feelings or the problems that had elicited them. She felt lost.

And stupid! Yes, she felt stupid!

And alone…she couldn't talk to anyone. Not her mother, definitely not her father, not Cal, and she had no friends to call. Sure, there were lots of ladies she was friendly with, but they were not 'real' friends, the kind you could blurt out all your fears, guilt and insecurities to. She had lost those friends after college, when everyone seemed to go their separate ways. In a way she had not needed anyone till now. Painfully she admitted to herself that Cal had been her best friend the last twenty years. She could always talk to him about anything. Didn't mean that he would always be listening or really interested in what she was saying, but he was there.

She felt a sharp pain in her chest.

She needed to do something.

She needed to go, she needed to get out. She grabbed her bag and ran out the door, stomping heavily all the way to town, never looking up once.

Seated at the diner counter, she ordered a huge 'Pancake Supreme' which consisted of a stack of pancakes topped with pecans, whipped cream and chocolate sauce, butter on the side, two scrambled eggs and three sausage links. She asked for a large coffee which she sweetened excessively and requested a slice of strawberry cheesecake for dessert. After all, she could always take it to go if she didn't eat it.

The matronly lady who ran the diner with her husband eyed her suspiciously,

"You alright, dear?"

"Of course"

"I guess you are just really hungry this morning, huh?

"I had a rough night, so yeah, I could eat a horse right now"

"Uh-huh, I can see that…did you have the allergies? Cos your eyes, they are quite red."

"They are? I…um…"

"It's ok, dear" She patted Beth's hand and smiled at her, "…it's on the house today…eat and drink whatever you want and as much as you want. It may hit the waistline, but sometimes it does make us girls feel better." Then she hurried to the kitchen.

The food arrived.

She stared at it and realized that she could not eat it.

With her stomach all tied up in a knot of emotions, she had no appetite whatsoever.

Tears threatened.

She got up to leave, rushing for the door.

"Hey, Miss!" the young waitress called after her.

"It's okay, let her go" said the owner.

✍

Bethany walked down Main Street trying to compose herself. Her vision was blurred because of the tears that filled her eyes and she did everything she could not to blink because then the tears would roll down her cheeks, and she really didn't want that. She stepped into the grocery store and asked for the bathroom.

Hot tears were washed away by a splash of cold water from the faucet and when she felt she could face the world again, she decided that since she was already here, some grocery shopping was in order.

Studying the different kinds of meats in the refrigerator, she was distracted by the loud voices of a group of women coming up behind her. Recognizing them, she froze.

"...ooh child, ain't that the truth..." came the hearty voice of Sister Toni. It was a bunch of women from church. What on earth were they doing here? And more importantly, how could she get the hell away from them?

"...but she was looking good, all things considered..." They continued their boisterous chatter and did not seem to notice her standing there. Even if they did see her, they probably would not recognize her, Beth thought to herself relieved. They'd only ever seen her dressed conservatively for Church, never in shorts. Slowly she leaned down and placed her shopping basket on the floor and without turning around, began to inch towards the nearest aisle. Once in the aisle, she took off running as fast as she could, out of the aisle, out of the store and out of town.

She'd been running at a fast and steady pace when she ran out of breath in front of the farm with the old woman sitting in front. She stopped, put her hands on her knees and tried to control her breathing. Her chest hurt. She had not run like this since she did some sprinting in high school. In college, she had adapted a slower pace and did some long distance running now and again, nothing too routine or regular.

"You alright there?" came the voice of the old woman. She was standing now, watching Beth from the distance.

Beth waved and nodded, signaling she was fine, and once her breath had evened out a little, she began a fast walk heading home.

With a few yards left and her house in view, she began to run again.

Something had happened to her during the sprint earlier. Something seemed to have awakened. Not spiritual or emotional, but purely physical. Her legs, her arms, her abs, they all seemed to chime together saying "That felt good. Do it again" and she obeyed.

She felt hot, sweaty and flushed. Her heart felt as though it were beating at least four times its normal rate. Her breathing was rapid and all her muscles tingled.

Standing with her keys in her hand about to open the front door, she felt her body taking over. She looked back over her shoulder and saw the neighboring field spreading out into the distance. She took the key out of the lock, let her bag fall to the ground in front of the door and walked to the gate staring over it as the fresh green hues of the field beyond summoned her. She took a deep breath, still recovering from her run home.

"I still got it in me" she affirmed, opened her gate and ran to the low fence that surrounded the field. She climbed over it easily and began to run. Fast then slow, then fast again, whatever her heart and lungs could take. She just ran. Aimlessly. In circles for all she cared. She just ran. She ran till she just couldn't anymore and then she let herself fall onto the grass and rolled in it, coming to a stop on her back, looking at the sky and breathing very hard.

All of her was hurting. Inside and out. She began to cry, letting the tears roll down the sides of her face.

She began to sob.

She began to shout. No words. Just emotion.

She could not pin point the particular reason she was crying. Out here, surrounded by green grass in a field she was trespassing on, she was just 'letting it out'. Whatever *it* was.

And it felt good.

Cleansed, she dragged herself home.

Her heart felt lighter, her mind felt clearer. There had been a shift somewhere inside her.

The following morning, she sat with her cup of tea in the seating area upstairs calmly letting thoughts and memories run through her head in no particular order or direction.

Her eyes travelled over the wall in front of her and she noticed the terrible job of wallpapering that had been done. Wanting a closer examination, she pulled away the seat that blocked her view of the lower part of the wall. She could now see that behind the chair it was not even real wall paper. It was more like white shelf liner that had been put up to hide some kind of mess beneath. Curious, she ripped off the paper.

What was hidden beneath was a colorful collection of splotches of paint, as if someone had just thrown their paint boxes at the wall.

"Oh my God!..." she whispered, remembering it immediately, "… Splashes of Happy!"

She must have been about nine or ten. She loved to color and paint. Coloring books and sketch pads were great, but she thought the plain white wall could use some decorating. She filled little bottle caps with various colors of paint from her paint box and splashed them on to the wall. The splotches ran into each other creating what she thought was the most beautiful work of art she had ever made. She had named it "Splashes of Happy" and was standing proudly before it when her father came up the stairs. Not even a little impressed, he exploded. Mad that she had painted on the wall and more mad that she really thought she could have a future with Art.

It was an ugly scene and it put an end to her artistic endeavors, because he seized all her art tools and forbade her to waste any more time on such "stupid frivolity", instructing her to spend her time more productively instead. He taught her to garden and grow her own food. This at least could feed her.

Like the memory of the event itself, she had buried her love for Art deep and far away inside her and had never let it resurface. Until now.

Here, standing in front of her childish mess, a desire stirred within her to paint again. Hadn't she seen an art supply store on Main Street? She knew where she was heading.

The afternoon sun reflected off a canvas mounted on an easel facing the front window. Palettes, tubes of paint, a variety of brushes, two rolls of canvas and a few large sketch pads lay on the floor. An open shopping bag from "Dunham Art Supplies" lay at the bottom of the stairs.

The house was silent, except for Bethany's breathing. Deep, excited and nervous.

She stood in front of the now fully exposed white wall of the seating area, a big paint brush in her hand. At her feet stood six cans of brightly colored paint. She stared at the wall with the intensity of a runner at the start of a race. She rolled the handle of the brush nervously in her hand and then with the words "We can always cover it with wallpaper" she dipped the brush into the yellow paint and drew a large bright streak on to the white wall. She stepped back and looked at it. "Well, can't stop now!"

She reached out the brush and drew another streak. And then another.

With each streak, she felt less nervous and more free.

She let go. And the emotions followed.

She painted and painted, turning the wall more and more yellow and as she painted, she could feel herself connecting to a part of herself she had not acknowledged in years. It was a part of herself she had shut away and locked up a long time ago but still recognized.

She painted furiously. Channeling all her anger through the brush and on to the wall.

She painted sadness. She painted all her disappointment in herself on to that wall. She was a failure. And she hated herself. And she had no idea what she was to do with herself or her life.

She was lost.

And the wall was yellow.

She fell on to a chair sweating, exhausted and brimming with realization.

"It was me all along. I screwed up! I am a loser! I suck. I gave up a long time ago. It was me. I fucked up."

With the gates to her soul open, she ventured back farther than she usually dared when she was riding on emotion. She went back to her mother's pain knowing she had been repeatedly betrayed; She felt her own pain, when her father turned against her desires and denied her the opportunity to get into a foremost fine art high school; She felt the pain of losing Nefertiti and the anger that followed setting her against Calvert even though she had denied it; She felt the blandness of her 'perfect' married life since then and she could see that she had buried all her pain in its 'perfection' and never truly dealt with it.

Cal was right. She had not been wholly present in their marriage for some time now.

She had blamed him, but she was just as much to blame.

The only relationship she was totally committed to was the one she had with her son, whom she could shower unrestrained with all her love and did with no hesitation. But the catch was, he was her son. A young man ready to live his own life. He was not betraying her trust, he was standing up for what he believed in and he was making his own choices.

Something she had never consciously done.

He was his own person. Something she had never been.

She stood up re-energized, picked up a new brush, dipped it into the orange paint, and approached the yellow wall.

"Hi Stoney, you are probably still asleep after a late night, but I want this to be the first call you get this morning! I want you to know that I am not mad at you. What I really mean to say is that I am proud of you. And I am happy for you and Jaden and I support you in your… adventure. I just…well, I am your Mom. You can expect me to worry and be concerned about your future and all, but I realize that I have to trust that you are a responsible young man and…well… I just wanted to say, I support you. Ok? Call me from time to time…if you like. I love you. Bye."

Beth felt as though she had a new lease on life. She had set Winston loose and decided that she was finally ready to have a conversation with Cal. She was not expecting an instant miraculous turn around, but she was ready to begin the process.

She'd been to town, had taken what was now a routine daily run and was just clearing up in the kitchen when there was a knock at the front door.

A knock at the door? She thought to herself confused. *No one knows I am here…except…Mom?*

She opened the door cautiously. It was an older gentleman in a gray suit.

"Mrs. Bethany Lambeau?"

"Yes"

"Delivery!" He handed her a large sealed envelope. "You have been served! Have a nice day"

She opened her mouth to speak, but nothing came out. She just stared after the man as he got in his car and drove off.

8

"Divorce."
"Divorce!"
"Divorce?"

She tried saying it every which way to see if it would sound less or more real.

She was in a state of shock and disbelief. Yes, she had moved out. Yes, she said she needed space and time. Yes, she had not been the friendliest or most welcoming since she'd left. But divorce??? She hadn't thought *that* far ahead.

They hadn't even discussed anything yet. How could he jump to such a final conclusion so fast?...and without her?

She'd have to call him to stop it.

But no! No way was she going to beg if this was what he wanted. She had pride!

Inside her head she could hear her own voice admonishing her; after all, he had wanted to talk from the beginning, it was she who had avoided it at all cost...yes...at *all* cost...it just cost her the whole thing. Her marriage was over.

Her little she-devil came to her rescue; after all, he was probably just waiting for a chance to get rid of her dead weight so that he could go out and get what he really wanted. Professor Marla Miralta, Latin Goddess! Fuck her! And Fuck him!

She slammed a fist on the table and marched up the stairs to her bedroom.

She wanted to call her mother, but she knew what she would say; "I told you so" "You should have gone back to him. Now you have lost everything"

She-devil had her own ideas about that too; *Yeah, but how did Cal know where to send the papers??? Mom!!!*

"She was in on it all along" she deduced aloud.

No, she was not calling her mother.

She was on her own. She had to think this through, and figure out what to do. She paced to and fro trying but unable to maintain a sensible stream of thought.

She noticed herself in the mirror and stood still. She thought it strange that she felt so strange. No crying, no angry outburst. How was she so…numb?

She shrugged.

"Only one thing for a girl to do when she's been dumped," Beth said out loud grabbing her purse, "go to the beauty parlor!"

Aaah….there is something so soothing about having yourself pampered. It's easy enough to do everything yourself, but to have someone do it for you makes you feel special. Makes you feel good. Makes you feel like you are worth it.

These were the thoughts going through Beth's mind as she lay back having her hair washed.   She was not one to venture into beauty parlors she was not accustomed to, in fact she been going to the same two places for the last decade. So being in this new environment meant being out of her comfort zone. But it was clean and well kept, the seats were comfortable and the ladies seemed nice enough. There was boisterous conversation going on, the latest music in the background and a TV on mute showing the headlines on CNN. Though she was welcomed by the clientele and dressers alike, it was clear that Beth was the stranger here. Everyone seemed to know everything about everyone else.

Champagne, the lady attending to her, was dark skinned and had a long well styled weave of solid black waves all the way down to her waist. Her eyes were exquisitely made up, with fine eyeliner, perfectly applied lashes and a glowing neutral shade of eye shadow. Her lips were a glossy espresso that just called for a kiss. Her nails were long and brightly colored, causing them to stand out against her dark skin. But what stood out the most, were her breasts which she seemed to have no qualms about emphasizing as her push up bra very nearly pushed them right out of her clingy black lace top. She was not a skinny girl by any means, but was so perfectly proportioned, that her ample bosom were just the perfect match for her equally ample behind which enjoyed just as much emphasis in a pair of tight-fitting black jeans. Bethany stared at her as she combed the tangles out of her long wet hair and admired how, even knowing that so much of this woman was cleverly applied and unreal, she was still beautiful.

She was watching Champagne's glossy lips moving in the mirror when she realized that she was talking to her,

"Girlfriend, I asked if you want a trim...your ends look like they need it"

"Yeah, sure...go ahead" She knew she was right because it had been ages since her last trim.   As Champagne prepared for it, Beth tuned in to the ongoing conversation.

A chubby light skinned lady with a conditioning cap on her head was just saying...

"...and don't you know, while she was at work, paying all them bills, his ungrateful self was gettin' fresh with the lady next door..."

The listeners made all the appropriate noises of shock and disgust.

"...talkin' 'bout how he working on his business from home,"

More sounds of disgust.

"Yeah Right!...Well, he deserve what he got when she threw his ass right out and tol' him to go move in next door" Everyone burst into laughter.

"Child, you know you can't trust no man left 'lone at home" said another customer.

"Well, how is she doing?" asked one of the hair dressers.

"Oh, she alright! She pretty, she young, she gonna fine a good one yet."

"Please, she don't need no man! I've been there, done that, bought the t-shirt. I don't need no man in my space all the time just to make me happy. I get what I need when I want it and then he gots to keep it moving." said the same hairdresser with attitude.

"But honey, you can say that now cos you young and all, but when things don't look or work like they use to, there ain't gonna be no one knockin' at your door. And you gonna be ole and alone"

"yup... and that's fine...I'll be *alone*...but not *lonely*. I enjoy my company. I'll be just fine"

At this point, Champagne joined in,

"Well, I'm going to be honest with myself. I like to have my man with me. We good *to* each other and we good *for* each other. Not to say we ain't got problems. We fight them out like everybody else, and not to say he ain't never looked at another woman...that just makes for a bigger fight. But we're determined to work things out. It's been twelve years so looks like it's working."

"Yeah, Yeah, Champagne, we all know about your hot and steamy married life" There were snickers all round.

"I keep telling you ladies, it keeps your man, and it keeps you young. I don't keep myself like this for nothing, you know" She flaunted herself as she spoke.

"Yes, and we all know, you pop right out them clothes when he so much as look at you." more laughter.

"That's right! He's gotta know that this is his, and it's gotta look good and enticing. Like Candy. You gotta keep yourself irresistible.

Make him horny. If you keep him facing you, his dick is only pointing in one direction, yours." Loud laughter, oohs and aahs.

"Unless he got one of them curvy ones that lean to one side" Another loud burst of laughter,

"Champagne, it's not all about sex," said the lady with the conditioning cap, "I never had no weave in my hair, never wore no tight clothes and Harvey and me gonna be celebratin' fifty years ness month."

Bethany could barely take this conversation anymore. Everything led back to Cal. All the talk of cheating husbands and sex only meant one thing to her right now, and she was getting very miserable about it.

As Champagne ran a comb through her hair, she thought of Cal running his fingers through her hair, pulling at it while they were making love, playing with it as they lay in the afterglow….

"Cut it!" She said quietly.

"Sorry?" asked Champagne.

Beth looked at Champagne in the mirror, dead in her eyes and spoke clear and loud

"Cut it!"

"Well, I am giving you a big trim here, that should do fine"

"No, I want you to cut it…cut it all"

"What? Like…short?"

"Yes, I'm talking Halle Berry short…cut it all off"

"Are you sure?" Champagne looked totally perplexed.

"Girl, Champagne be puttin' in extensions and weaves to have hair as long as yours. You sure you wanna cut all that?" It was the other hairdresser.

"How your man gonna feel about that? They all want that long hair you know" said the lady with the conditioning cap.

"I could just give you a nice just-above-the-shoulder cut…then you'll still have some length to play with." said Champagne.

"No! I am serious! I want it cut! Please do it. Now!" She very nearly yelled.

Everyone was staring at Beth in shocked silence. She tried to play it off,

"I'm sorry….I just really, really want to cut it all off. I really need a new look, a drastic change"

"Champagne, go on an' cut the girl's hair. Can't you see there's somethin' goin' on there?" The wisdom of the elder in the conditioning cap had spoken. Everyone went back to what they had been doing and Champagne prepared to make the first cut.

"Shoot," mumbled the other hairdresser. "Champagne, you better make sure you make some clean cuts, might could use it as extensions for someone else"

Even Beth laughed at that one.

She'd had to cut it.

She literally had to get Cal out of her hair. And in that moment watching the hair he loved so much, fall to the floor with each snipping sound of the scissors, she made up her mind what to do. She was not going to sign the divorce papers. But she was not going to contest either. She had come out here for space and time and if he could not give her that after twenty years of marriage, then so be it. She knew now more than ever, that she needed this. She needed to find herself again. If, by what now seemed to be a high improbability, they were destined to get back together it would all play itself out that way. But it would be under new terms set by her new self. The very short hair she now strutted confidently down the street with was just the beginning. Her art was another rediscovery. And…hey, there was that guy again, raking someone's front yard. Somehow, it seemed his hair was a different color every time she saw him. Right now, against the sun, it shone bright reddish gold.

"Hey!" she called to him.

He turned toward her and came over looking somewhat confused until he got closer and recognition registered on his face,

"Wow!" he said when he reached her. He stared blatantly. Her hair, her face, her body.

She blushed, feeling embarrassed.

"Hello" she said a little coldly.

"Wow!" he repeated, slower and deeper, slowly shaking his head from side to side "You look… beautiful!…um…sorry…I…I hope you don't mind my saying."

"I can take a compliment" she said, more in an effort to convince herself, "Thank you"

"It's just…this hair cut…damn, you look hot!" he laughed, then waved his hands, "okay, no more, no more, I apologize, especially since this is the first time we are actually really talking. I shouldn't be so forward. Forgive me"

"Well, we haven't really started talking yet"

He chuckled, "Yeah, that's true" he suddenly looked somewhat shy and uncomfortable making her feel bad after all the nice things he'd said.

"Look, I've seen what you do, and I need some color in my yard"

"Boy, do you!" He seemed excited, "I would love to get my hands on your yard"

"I want to add a herbaceous border to the right. Something bright would really pop out back there maybe with some Lavatera or Hollyhocks in lavender and blue or maybe white. Phlox or Peonies, some Cranesbill, Coneflowers, that sort of thing. I also want an herb garden toward the back and I am thinking some kind of artsy rock garden with clay pots or such around the tree stump, but that'll come later. The flowers are the priority."

"I see you know some stuff"

"I used to work on that garden with my Dad so, yeah, I know a thing or two, but it's so far gone, I think I need some help to bring it back to life."

"No doubt" He was smiling that smile again. And she was feeling really weird about it.

"I take it you are interested?"

"Very! But can I make one *small* request?"

"Depends. What is it?

"Could I design it myself?...I mean, I know you have ideas already, and you know your plants and all, but your yard is like a whole new project. It's like painting a whole new masterpiece from scratch. That would give me the greatest pleasure" He looked like a kid excited about a new toy.

"Okay so you are speaking my language with the painting, but you sound really weird saying it would *'give you the greatest pleasure'*...what are you? Twenty?...I can imagine a myriad of other great pleasures someone of your age could look forward to."

"You paint?" he said obviously ignoring her last comment.

She felt a twinge of excitement being asked about her rediscovered passion, but she also felt she was not quite ready to open up about it yet so she tried to wave it off.

"Just getting back into it after a really long hiatus"

"That rocks!" he smiled but added seriously. "And then you should know what I mean."

There was a silent pause as they just looked at each other.

This was obviously very real to him and she did know what he meant.

Slowly, she nodded.

"Yes, yes I do! And you know what? You can make it your canvas, I got plenty of my own. I will need to approve the final design, but it can be yours. Knock yourself out!"

"Yes!!!" He pumped his fist and flashed his hugest smile yet.

"Can I come by tomorrow morning for a walk through? You can show me what you have in mind?" His excitement was infectious.

"Sure, fine! Any time after nine is good"

"Nine? Thought you were a late sleeper"

"What? Why?"

"Cos of the day you yelled at me for mowing the lawn *so early*"

"Well it *was* early. I was trying to sleep in" She argued.

"Hello? It was 2 p.m." He was looking really mischievous; probably enjoying that she was completely horrified and humiliated by this revelation. She wanted to sink into the earth and definitely cancel his work on her yard. But she said, "Look, 9 a.m. is fine. Good bye!" and without waiting for a response, she walked off knowing that he was standing there giggling to himself. And he was.

9

The next morning, she jumped out of bed with an extra burst of energy. She took a quick shower and threw on a t-shirt and a pair of sweats. Remembering his compliments the day before, she checked herself in the mirror to see if she could match them today.

Hmm, she thought as she examined her backside, *it's not as if I have a butt like Champagne's to show off.* Then she caught herself. What was she thinking? What did it matter what she wore? Compliments were nice, but please! It hardly mattered what he thought of her outfit. Now or at any other time. She went down to get some coffee and wait for him to arrive.

He was prompt. At nine o'clock she saw him at her gate.

"Come on in" She called to him from her front door, and then met him half way in the yard.

"Good Morning, Ms. Lambeau" He smiled.

"How'd you know my name?"

"I am the king of these here gardens, 'tis my business to know these things"

"No offense, but you are so weird" she laughed.

"None taken, I have heard that before"

"Yeah and Good Morning…???"

"Jake"

"Good Morning, Jake" She feigned a slight smile. He didn't say anything, but she noticed the quick once over he gave her and her inner flirt began to make a concerted effort to muscle herself out. Beth kept her in check, cleared her throat and turned to the yard.

"Follow me"

For almost an hour, they walked around the yard and talked about how they envisioned the space, what plants they favored and why, shared personal experiences related to gardening, and came up with a general game plan. It was going to be a dirty and arduous job, but it promised to be fun and an essential part of her new life.

As Bethany saw him off at the gate, she reflected on the pleasant time they had just spent. So many memories came back. Fond moments spent with her father. Things he had taught her that she thought were long forgotten with lack of use, came back to her clearly as they had talked. This weird young boy, who could be no older than her own son made her feel completely at ease…over gardening!

What followed were two weeks of childlike abandon for Beth.

Jake still had his other commitments, so there was plenty of down time for her to spend on her Art. She sketched and painted, spent time at the local library reading about methods and techniques, drove to the next town and spent entire days visiting museums and drawing anything that caught her interest. She had a lot of lost time to make up for.

When she sketched or painted, her mind was free.

Devoid of thought or worry.

Focused on the work in front of her, her subconscious took over and she felt free to create. If she had felt any heaviness, it was lifted.

The movements of her hand over the paper or canvas felt magical. There was no thought of how things should be, had to be, must be. Her hands would move, her soul would sing and there would be a completed piece of art in front of her. In all her years attending

Spirit-filled church services with Cal, she had never felt more close to God than she did now.

While she was creating, she felt as though she was in His very presence.

She could hear the Angels sing.

Sometimes, a song of praise would pop into her head and she would sing along. Other times, a Bible verse would inspire what she was creating and would lend a title to it. She had no idea or care for the quality of what she was doing. All that mattered was that she reveled in this her long lost love.

But it was not just her spirit that was being rejuvenated. Her body too was getting revitalized.

Every day began with a run and each day she would push herself just a little harder or further.

Then when Jake came over, she worked with him. Together they dug up the weeds and plants that had made themselves at home in the soil and created a compost pile behind the house. The soil was dry and hard to dig through and the roots had firmly entwined themselves in it which made uprooting and digging a solid work out. She ended every day exhausted and exhilarated.

Her phone lay on the dresser upstairs, suffering neglect. She had not called anyone nor had she checked any messages since the day the court papers arrived. She had not even read all the papers, but had put them back in the envelope and had placed the envelope safely on the top shelf of her wardrobe. There would be no use for it.

She called Winston from the public phone at the diner and he seemed to be doing fine. If anything *were* to happen, she knew Winston would call her mother and she would know how to reach her.

No need to worry.

Her freedom was complete.

The weather had been pleasant, but Jake felt it had been too dry and was hoping for rain. He wanted the soil to 'feed'. And finally, he got his wish.

It was early evening, but it looked dark and gloomy outside. It was not a 'Jake day', so she had been to town and back with nothing much else on the agenda for the night other than a cozy dinner and a glass of wine.

She was startled by a loud clap followed by a roll of thunder. The house got darker as the last traces of sunlight were devoured by the incoming storm. She stood at the window watching the sky as it moved and groaned, the large heavy gray clouds rolling in discomfort, pregnant and impatient to give birth.

She pondered why humans had attributed storms with negativity, when watching one was like watching nature at work; it was beautiful. Who could deny the miracle of a thunder storm?

There was another loud roll of thunder and in a sudden burst Mother Nature birthed her life giving bounty. The rain fell strong and heavy. Trees bowed at its force and as the ground was pelted repeatedly, water quickly gathered in puddles and formed rivulets that flowed in any direction that was open to them.

Turning away from the window, Beth turned on the radio to the smooth jazz station, and headed to the kitchen preparing to relax to a warm candle lit meal.

Her empty plate in front of her, she was just sipping her chardonnay when she thought she saw a movement outside. She turned off the one lamp that was on and tiptoed to the front window to take a look.

Sure enough, soaked from head to toe, he was digging in the front yard.

She ran to the front door and shouted out to him.

"Jake?"

"Oh, Hi!"

"What the hell are you doing out there? Are you crazy? You are going to make yourself sick. Come inside right now!" she commanded.

Laughing, he dropped everything and ran to the door.

"How long have you been out there?"

"A good while"

"Obviously! Look at you! You are drenched! This is ridiculous"

"It is so fun. You are at one with nature out there. You should try it sometime"

"I most certainly will not! Go to the kitchen, I'll get you a robe and dry your clothes"

She ran up the stairs and he obeyed, heading to the kitchen as he took in his surroundings.

"So you really do paint! This place looks like an artist's studio. Who'd have thought"

When she returned, he was standing deferentially in the center of the kitchen with his arms behind his back, like a little kid in the principal's office.

"Here!" She handed him a robe and a towel, "take those off, and leave them right there, put this on for now, I'll run your clothes through the dryer and you should be good to go home."

She turned and went back to sit at the dining table, facing the other way to ensure his privacy.

Slowly, dressed in the grey robe she'd given him, he stepped out in front of her.

"Thanks, I guess" he said shyly.

"Sit down. Do you want something to eat? Or drink?...I just ate, but there's plenty enough left if you are hungry."

"Sure! Thanks!" He sat down.

She placed a plate of salmon stir-fry with a side of greens and wild rice in front of him.

"Wow! It's *real* food"

"What were you expecting?"

"A sandwich. That's what I usually get when I am offered something to eat"

"Okay, I'll remember that for next time. Something to drink?"

"Could I just have water and some of this wine you are drinking?"

"Sure. No problem"

Once he was settled and eating with gusto, she went back to the kitchen to dry his clothes.

As was habitual, she shook out the jeans and reached into the pockets to make sure they were empty. He had left his wallet in his back pocket. She pulled it out, put it down on the top of the dryer and continued to put his t-shirts into the dryer. She set the timer, turned the dryer on and picked up the wallet to bring to him at the table. Seeing him focused on his meal, mischief and curiosity got the better of her. She turned away from him and opened his wallet to examine its contents. No sooner had she done so, something green fell out and to the floor. She looked at him. He hadn't noticed. She quickly bent down to pick it up. It was a condom. She gasped, embarrassed. Why was it that every time she was nosy, she found condoms? She quickly put it back into the wallet and gave up on any further investigation. At least he practiced safe sex, she thought as she returned to the table, hopefully Winston did the same.

"Your wallet was in your pocket. It's pretty wet too"

"Oh, thanks." He indicated the food, "This is great. Thanks so much"

"Glad you are enjoying it." She sat down across from him, poured him a glass of wine, and watched him as he ate.

In the dim light, he looked darker than he usually did. His hair which appeared brown when wet was beginning to dry in wild golden curls around his head. She marveled yet again at how hard it was to identify the actual color of his hair. Depending on the position of the sun or whatever light it reflected, it could appear golden, red or dark blond. The color of his eyes was just as hard to place. She tried to remember what they usually looked like. Grayish green? Or were they greenish gray? Ridiculous! She'd have to take a better look the next time she worked the yard with him. He was unshaven. Not something Cal would do. Cal was always clean shaven but she had to admit that his stubble gave Jake an attractively macho air. And his lips. Well, Cal had much fuller lips, there was no denying that, but Jake's lips did have potential. Potential? Potential for what? She laughed at herself mentally as she noticed herself gently biting on her lower lip, and concluded that though Jake was certainly pleasing to the eye, he was the "un-Cal". That's what she would call him. "The Un-Cal". He could not compete.

"So…um…Where is Mr. Lambeau?"

"'Scuse me?" She was certain he had been reading her mind. She blushed.

"Well, I was just wondering, you are a beautiful woman, a good cook and we both know you are married…so…why are you living in your garden retreat alone?"

"Maybe I am taking an artist retreat" she threw at him defiantly.

"Maybe" he nodded and watched her intently as he took a sip of his wine. She felt convinced that the word 'liar' was printed boldly on her forehead the way he was looking at her.

"You know, it's really not your business, but if you must know, we are temporarily separated."

"Hmmm" he nodded again and stared at his glass. "I am truly sorry to hear that."

"Thanks"

"And I hope you get to work it out" he searched her eyes. "…if that's what you want"

"I don't really know what I want right now," Beth scoffed. "I guess that's why I am here"

Immediately she'd said it, she regretted her honesty. What was she telling this guy all this for? She'd better stop with the wine before she let out too much.

"That makes sense. Sometimes taking time off helps you refocus. I get that."

"Oh, do you?" She asked and held her tongue to avoid saying more than was necessary.

"Yeah, I took a time out when I was figuring out what I really wanted to do with my life."

"Gardening?" She maintained her caution.

"Nah, I am a pre-med sophomore at Washington East"

"A Doctor? You? But you have such a thriving business going here and you are so good at it. I would have thought you had a love for gardening."

"I do! But it also serves a bigger purpose. The business is putting me through school and also…I am not a big people person. So I'll always come back to the garden for peace."

"I hate to have to break it to you, but being a doctor is a people job. And what do you mean *you are not a people person*? You are such a nice friendly guy!"

He laughed taking a sip of his wine, "Well, I didn't say I wasn't a nice guy or that I don't know how to get along with people, I just don't want to have to get too intimate with them" he leaned forward, getting serious, "Thing is…Plants are easy. It takes water, a little TLC and you can be sure that they'll respond the way you know they will and they always reward you with beauty. People? Takes a whole lot more than water and nurturing with them and they still disappoint and hurt you. You just can't put your faith in them." He stared into his glass and she could tell he'd been hurt.

"I know what you mean" she commiserated.

"But it's the art of practicing Medicine that draws me. Understanding how it all works, understanding what can go wrong, figuring out how to fix it, coming up with a treatment plan and implementing it, while maintaining comfort and trust. That, to me, is genius." His sincerity was clear, his passion obvious. It warmed her heart and she could not help staring into his eyes, moved by their intensity.

"And you know what? I think you're gonna be great at it."

"I know! I never do anything half ass"

Typical young man, she thought, *so cocky!*

"So what happened? Some girl broke your heart and now you don't trust people?" Her blunt attack was intended to knock him off his high horse.

"Not *some girl*, my mother" he responded calmly, and Beth was off her own horse and in the dust.

"Oh!" she fumbled. "I'm sorry…um…what happened?"

"Let's just say we had a difference of opinion about her lifestyle. But we are all good now."

"You made up?"

"Nope, we just don't talk." He shrugged looking straight at her. "You know, you are really pretty when you look at me like that."

As they looked at each other, him gloating over his victory as he sat erect and proud on his steed still brandishing his weapon, and her dusting herself off from her fall, she could feel the heat rising between them.

She had to stop it! She would have to get away from him as quickly as possible and change the subject to bring some semblance of reality back into this conversation. She stood up with a start, picking up their plates.

"Well, I hope my son Winston wakes up to his future after his time off as nicely as you have done" she threw over her shoulder as she headed to the kitchen.

He seemed totally unchanged remaining calm, friendly and interested. How dare he stay that way while her blood was rushing through her in heated torrents?

"Really? What is he doing?"

"Touring with some electronic djs or something. He does interactive program designs and installations."

"Get out! That's hot!"

"I'd expect that from you. That's what all you young folks are into, isn't it?"

"Hey, why do you always emphasize how *young* I am?"

"Well, it's a fact, isn't it?"

"But why do you keep bringing it up? Ever heard the saying that 'age is nothing but a number'?"

"Yes, I have. And that number usually gives a pretty good idea of where a person's mind is at"

"Oh yeah? Ok, so I am twenty-five…tell me where my mind is at"

"Are you?"

"uh huh, go ahead! I want to know where my head is at."

"Really? Well, I thought you were younger when you said you were a sophomore."

"Does it win me brownie points that I am a few years older than you thought?" he smiled.

"No, you are still just six years older than my own son, so I would say that you are probably still a little unstable and uncertain about life, still figuring yourself out."

"Ah, but the fact is; I have been on my own since I was seventeen? I worked through the end of high school, started my own gardening business and have been self-sufficient since then. No parents got me here, I did this on my own and when I got a clear idea of what I wanted to do with my life, I got myself into college and will work my way through that too."

"Well, so, I guess you are not the typical young adult. Well done!"

"AND you read me wrong, Ms. Lambeau." He stood up and began making his way to the kitchen, "I *am* stable, I *am* certain about life and I *have* pretty much figured myself out. I have a solid idea of what I want and what I have to do to get it. So I believe the saying is true – Age is…"

She could feel him coming up behind her,

"…nothing but a number" she finished the sentence as she turned to face him.

"Exactly" he said now standing right in front of her smirking. He was so close, she could smell what deodorant was left on him from his working in the rain. Her eyes moved from his face down his neck and to his chest, exposed just enough as the robe hung loosely over his shoulders. She could see it rise and fall with his breathing and all her primal instincts urged her to get closer, to touch him, no, to *grab* him.

"Yes, yes I guess you have a point." She turned from him and opened the dryer, "Anyway, your clothes are dry, here you go!" She shoved his clothes at him and hurriedly pushed past him out of the kitchen, "Seems the rain has stopped and it's getting a little late."

"Right. Thanks" He watched her leave and then let the robe fall off his shoulders.

When she was a distance she considered safe enough away from him, she turned around only to catch sight of him standing in his boxers as he prepared to put his clothes back on. She could barely breathe. His body was beautiful and the desire that washed over her was undeniable. She felt her sweat pores come to life. This was dangerous territory, very dangerous. Tearing her eyes off him, she rushed to the front door and waited for him there.

"Hey you know what we should do?" he was saying, "We should go to the flower show in Oldesville next week."

She cleared her throat trying to compose herself and sound normal,

"Flower show?"

"Yeah, it's great. It'll give us a chance to look through some plants you might want to get. It's right next to the fair ground, so we could make a day of it. It'll be fun. Whaddaya say?"

He was coming out of the kitchen now.

"I don't really like fairgrounds or markets, but I guess the flower show could be good. Ok, yes. Sure, we can go"

He looked around again as he walked through the living room toward her,

"When do I get to see some of your art work? It's only fair, you've seen most of mine"

He was smiling his smile again.

"Not today," she opened the door, "Good night!"

He got the message and began heading out but stopped right in front of her. She stepped back and tried to get as much of the door between them as was possible.

"Hey, Thanks for the food and all, it was really nice talking with you."

"Uh huh, no problem." She kept her eyes on the floor.

"See you tomorrow?"

Oh God, did she need to? She wished she would never see him again, "Yeah sure."

"Looking forward to it. Good night!"

She was so scared that he was going to try something, but he just walked right out.

"Yeah, Good night!" she said and closed the door right behind him without even checking to see if he had any means of getting home.

She stood behind the door, breathing hard. She didn't dare to look out the windows in case he was still out there and she didn't want to walk back to the kitchen because if he *was* out there, he might be watching and might see how unstable she was on her feet right now. What the devil was that about? What was going on? But she knew. It had been years since she had felt this, but she knew very well what it was. No, the question was not 'what was it?'

The question was 'what was she going to do about it?'

10

They agreed to meet at the fountain in the square on Main Street. Bethany would drive.

She saw him as she approached and watched him while she stood at a red light. He was leaning against a lamp post, drinking from a paper cup. He was wearing jeans and sneakers, a white t-shirt and had a casual Roca Wear leather jacket thrown over his left shoulder. She could tell that he'd had a haircut and a shave. He looked totally at ease…and good.

She was fifteen minutes late because even as she got herself ready, she had had reservations about this trip. Not just about being with him all day, but she really was not a fan of crowded fairgrounds and market places. Couldn't they just have gone to a botanical garden instead?

The light turned green and she moved forward pulling up by him. He smiled, threw his cup into a nearby trash can and ran to the car.

"Mornin'" he said jumping in excitedly.

"Mornin'" she replied.

Looking at her, he could tell she did not mirror his excitement.

"Don't worry," he said. "We'll have fun"

"Yeah, right!" she said doubtfully. "Can we just have a contingency plan so that if I *really* don't like it, we can leave?"

"We won't need that plan, but ok!...come on! Where is your sense of spontaneity?"

"Probably at the maternity ward of St. Luke's" she joked, but somewhere deeper, it hit a true note. She fell silent for a moment and in just that amount of time, traveled from realization, through sadness and disappointment and finally to determination…it was time to live again.

"Come on, let's go!"

"Alright!!! That's what I'm talking about" he laughed slapping his knee, and away they drove.

The Oldeville Recreational Field had been an air field for small and medium sized planes in the 1930's. In fact, the highway that led to it used to be a runway.

A portion of the tarmac served as the car park and beyond that one could see huge white tents and beyond that, a Ferris wheel, roller coaster and other indications of an amusement park.

The tents that housed the flower show were adorned with garlands and wreaths and large posters and bill boards showing a wide variety of plants.

Contrary to what she had expected, she did not feel uncomfortable at all.

Though there were many people, it was not too crowded to get around, see what there was to see and have conversations with the merchants. Beth and Jake bought a few plants and seeds and by the time they'd been through the entire expanse of the three large tents, Beth had completely caught on to Jake's excitement about the day and the show and was shocked to find that they had spent the entire early part of the day there. It was about two o'clock and standing at the edge of the last tent, holding two bags of purchases, she declared she was hungry.

"There's a really good pizza stand inside the fair, we could grab a bite there"

"Okay!" she said with no hesitation what so ever about going into the Amusement Park.

As they wandered through the park, they looked at the rides and laughed as they watched riders screaming in the downward drop of a thrill ride.

"Oh my God, I would just die on those things" Beth said. "I haven't been on a roller coaster since I was in my twenties"

"Dare you!"

"Heck, no! Let's just go get the pizza"

"Ok! Hey, let me have those" he grabbed her bags and suddenly disappeared into the crowd.

She stood looking after him confused but didn't want to move in case they lost each other. So she waited.

Within minutes, he was back, without bags and a hand full of tickets.

"What the..???"

"Bags are safely in a locker and we are going on a thrill ride"

"Aaaahh…no, we're not" she shook her head vigorously.

"Pick one Ms. Lambeau! We are going to do it."

Laughing uncontrollably, she chose 'The Tornado', a relatively tame roller coaster.

The whole way to the ride she was laughing with tears in her eyes.

"I so cannot do this, Jake. I really can't. I might die on the way or at least have a heart attack"

"Then you'll be my first ever patient to try CPR on" he joked as they got to the ticket taker who was watching their tug of war with bored disinterest.

"Are you getting on or not?" the ticket taker asked.

"Yes, we are" announced Jake handing over the tickets and he pulling her in, getting into the nearest car.

"Oh my God, oh my God…" she kept screaming. "I am gonna die, I just know it…Jake, I am gonna hate you for a really long time for this…a really, really long time"

He just kept laughing.

They were buckled in and the ride took off.

She did survive it.

With her eyes squeezed shut, pushing her legs into the floor of the car as hard as she could, screaming and grabbing tightly on to Jake who had his arms up in the air, hollering and laughing the whole way as if he was riding down the freeway in a convertible.

They stumbled off the ride in fits and she held on the nearest wall doubling over laughing. He held her to support her.

Finally, the laughter began to subside

"You ok?" he asked.

"Yes…it was crazy, but it was fun"

"Wanna go again?"

She threw him a playful punch to the chest and gave him a mean look.

"Oooh, scary" he said laughing. He pulled her in making moves to head over to the Pizza stand, but as she came close to him, before she could catch herself, she planted a kiss on his lips.

He stopped in his tracks, responding deliberately before she could change her mind, kissing her fully and deeply. The arm he had around her pulled her in just a little closer. She enjoyed the feel of his tongue against hers, her lips were completely in his, and though she could feel his body get tenser with each moment, his hold and kiss remained gentle.

They stared at each other as their lips came apart.

His eyes looked so dark right now, she felt like she could see all the way into his soul and his soul was calling to hers. She wanted to let herself go and fall into their deep longing. She wanted his arm around her to press her even closer to him. She wanted his other arm to reach for her head and pull her close for another kiss. A more passionate hungry desperate and downright arousing kiss. Yes, that is what she wanted. But wait…what was she thinking???

She pulled herself away with a start.

"I am so sorry" she mumbled shaking her head. "I am sorry"

"I'm not" his voice and gaze were warm and steady. His smile, very slight.

"Oh Jake…I really…I …this is no good…we gotta go, we gotta go" She turned, pulling herself away from him and quickly walked away.

"We'll just get the Pizza" he called after her.

"No! This is not good, Jake…I don't know where you think this is going, but it can't go there. It just can't. We have to go. Please get our bags, and meet me at the car"

"Ok" he said more to himself as he watched her go.

The drive back was an awkwardly quiet one. She concentrated hard on the road and said nothing except repeating how crazy she must be every now and then. He rode shotgun and said nothing.

Pulling up at the fountain on Main Street. She stopped the engine and turned to face him;

"Jake, I did not mean for that to happen and I will not let it happen again." she started out firmly, "You are a nice guy and all, but I am married and well…I am old enough to be your mother. I just…I can't do this." He just watched her and listened, remaining quiet.

She continued with some hesitation, "I think it will be best if you finish the garden on your own. And after it's done, I don't think it is a good idea for you to come back. I will maintain it myself. Do you understand what I mean?"

He took a deep breath and nodded, "Wow! I didn't think you felt that bad about it. But if that's what you want…"

"It's really for the best, Jake"

"It's for the best?" he repeated. "What I asked you is if that is what you want. Wrong answer!"

She took her eyes away from him looking out at the street in front of her and answered,

"It *is* what I want!"

"Clear! Got it! Alright then, take care" he got out of the car and walked away without as much as a backward glance.

She sat watching him for a few minutes breathing deeply. She knew she had done the right thing and when she got home, she headed straight upstairs, threw herself on the bed and hugged her pillow tight telling herself how relieved she was about the fate she had just avoided.

Yet, she found guilty enjoyment in imagining the fate that could have been, had she not avoided it.

11

In the days that followed, whenever he was at work in her garden, she either made sure that she was out or otherwise occupied.

On his part, he worked diligently as usual. He whistled along to the music playing on his earphones as he worked. He was oblivious to her, present or not. It seemed he had accepted her decision completely, staying to himself and leaving at the end of the day, with no good bye, no smile, nothing.

A week had passed since the trip to Oldeville. The new flowers had been nicely rooted into their new home in Bethany's front yard and Jake was adding some layers of perennials to add an immediate flare to the garden.

She watched him from the window. His tee-shirt could not hide the muscles on his back. His sweat pants hung casually on his butt. He was busy fiddling with something in his hand and had no idea she was watching him.

She, on the other hand, was watching intently. She chewed on a fingernail as she thought about the implications of what she had in mind. She opened the front door;

"Hey Jake," she called out to him, "I am ready"

"Excuse me?" He turned looking confused.

"I am ready to show you my art work"

"Oh!" A non-chalant response and with a shrug he turned back to what he was doing.

"I'm trying to build up enough confidence to show my work,"

"Uh huh"

"…so I wonder if I could have your opinion on some of it"

"It's not like I am an art expert or anything" He was not making this easy.

"Yes, I know…but…well, you could still look at it from the point of view of a potential buyer"

"Guess I could" he mumbled without turning around.

She waited a few minutes for a further response and not getting any, she gave up and turned to go back in. Just as she was about to close the door he threw a statement over his shoulder,

"I'll come in when I am done for the day…soon"

"Ok. Thanks!"

Nervous now that he had accepted her invitation, she retreated into the house not knowing where to start. She quickly put out some fruit, nuts, cheese and wine and tidied up the living room a little bit. Then she paced to and fro, walking in and out of the kitchen aimlessly.

Finally, he knocked at the door.

"It's open!" she called out positioning herself behind one of the dining table chairs.

He came in, looking around casually.

"Hi" she smiled.

"Hi" he replied.

"How've you been?"

He looked at her quizzically "Could I just freshen up a bit?"

"Oh, sure…you know your way around"

Watching her carefully, he walked into the kitchen, turned on the faucet and prepared to wash his face and hands.

She tried to force herself to relax.

"So…what's up?" he asked.

"Ah…well, I wondered how you were"

"Nice of you. I am fine. You?"

"Ok…been keeping busy"

"Aha! Always a good thing"

"Yeah" she laughed nervously and indicated the spread on the table, "would you like a snack or some wine?"

"Like a real art reception…wine and cheese. That's funny"

"I guess it is. Here, this wine is really good and it goes very well with the cheese. And then I guess I can start to show you around"

"Uh hun…Ok" he accepted the glass from her and was about to drink.

"Wait" she stopped him, "let's make a toast…a toast to new beginnings"

"Ok, whatever!" he shrugged.

"I guess I just feel weird about the other day. We had so much fun and then I guess I ended the day in a kind of drastic fashion. I want to apologize and I would really like it if we could sort of…start over."

He seemed amused, "You are lonely out here, aren't you?"

"A little"

"…and you were scared that day"

"A lot"

"…and that is your solution to everything?"

"what?"

"You run away"

"I…er…now you sound like my husband."

"Oh! Well, I really don't want to do that. We're good. Here," he raised his glass, "to new beginnings! Cheers!"

They clicked glasses and sipped their wine each trying to read the others thoughts.

"Ok," he broke the silence first, "let's see what you've got…"

"Ok…let's start here," she led him to her most recent piece which she had done the day after they had been to the fair. It echoed all her confusion, desires and fears in an array of dark colors interspersed with streaks of light blue, like a clear sky trying to alight from behind a cloudy day.

"Hmm" he said examining it closely while she examined him closely. "I think I like it, but it's too dark and heavy looking. Doesn't really speak to me"

"Interesting" she said and showed him another dark colored painting. It seemed to make him smile,

"I like that one better. It's the lines, I think. I don't know, but I like that one better even though it's dark too"

"Really interesting! It's like you can sense the mood I was in when I painted these, because the first came out of turmoil and this came out of tranquility"

"That *is* interesting, isn't it?" he said looking at her.

"Now I'm going to want to show you all my stuff just to see if that was a coincidence"

"Go for it"

She launched into a presentation of all the paintings and sketches she had been doing since she came out to The Farm. He asked earnest and intelligent questions and she described and explained whatever he wanted to know. Even though he was her one viewer, her confidence in her work took a quantum leap.

They ended up sitting at the table emptying the wine and munching on the fruit and cheese, drifting from one topic of conversation to another with ease and comfort.

"You know, it's getting kinda late" he said looking at the clock. "I should be heading out"

"Yeah, ok, I guess so"

He grabbed an apple from the tray, "I'll take this for the road"

"Sure. No problem. Hey, can you hold on a minute? I'll be right back" she said and ran up the stairs before he could answer.

He waited patiently, entertaining himself by taking a second look at some of the artwork.

Then she called from upstairs.

"By the way, there is one more piece up here. I painted the whole wall. Come take a look!"

Taking a bite of his apple, he walked leisurely to the stairs and made his way up. Almost at the top, he came across her "Streaks of Happy" and stood back taking it in as a whole.

"Heeey, I like this one" he called out with his mouth full.

He took the last steps up taking a closer look at the wall.

"I don't know if you'd like to look at this one too…"

On the verge of taking another bite out of his apple, he turned to see her standing at the door of her bedroom, wearing only a robe draped loosely over her shoulders. She held the robe closed in front of her chest and let the rest of it fall lazily around her, leaving one leg exposed up to her thigh.

He stopped and stared at her. Then lowered the apple from his mouth, cleared his throat and managed to say, "Ms. Lambeau, I am sure you are well aware that it is not wise to tease."

He watched her intently but didn't move.

Fear began to set in as she thought for a moment that she was being rejected, but it was too late to turn back now. She took a deep breath lifting her chest, raised her head convincing herself that she was the femme fatale she was trying to be, and looking him dead in the eyes, in a voice as clear as she could muster, she said,

"I hardly have the time nor the mood for teasing, Mr. Blumenthal. You are either interested, as I believe you once were, or you are not."

"If I come over there, there'll be no turning back, Beth…last chance…I can leave"

"Oh, stop being such a gentleman, Jake. This isn't easy for me."

Her femme fatale melted and she looked away beginning to have serious second thoughts about this. But her body was speaking louder than any other part of her. Looking back at him, she let her robe fall off her shoulders and said,

"No turning back"

He crossed the distance between them in the space of the stunted breath that followed her words, kissing her feverishly. She began to tug at his tee-shirt. He pulled it off and as they continued kissing, he backed her into the bedroom.

They fell on to the bed, his kisses moving from her lips, to her neck, down her chest and to her breasts.

She fought hard to keep her thoughts about her. Telling herself what she should be feeling, making sure she was responding with the right intensity of moans and movement, but each minute made it harder to concentrate and when his lips closed around her nipple and she felt his tongue roll over and around it, all thought and control was lost.

In the moment she felt nothing but pure and absolute passion.

She allowed it to take complete control of her as she lay back and let him pleasure every part of her.

She heard herself moaning louder than she usually did, leaving scratch marks on his shoulder as she reached for him in her throws of a very near orgasm.

He stopped and stood looking down at her as he let his sweatpants drop, followed by his boxers.

She thought he was saying something to her. It sounded like "You are so beautiful" but she couldn't be certain if it was not her own voice saying it to him. His body was an impeccably carved sculpture and his perfect throbbing manhood was as eager as she was. She begged him to hurry as he ripped open the slim Trojan packet. And when he finally entered her, what little there was left of her senses took flight, soaring beyond rhyme and reason, gliding over a horizon of ardor, into the brilliance of an orgasmic sunrise. The bright yellow orange sun burst open and millions of bright yellow and orange birds flew out wildly in every direction chirping happily, creating a din that drowned out every other sound of nature.

The last of the birds disappeared in the distance and there was silence and a clear blue sky which slowly began to look more and more like the bedroom ceiling.

She was back.

12

He spent the night.

And a few more after that.

When they ran out of refrigerated left overs they were forced to admit that they could not exist on sex alone.

They took separate showers for the first time since their first night as they got ready to head into town to do some shopping.

They sat at lunch in O'Malley's, the local Irish pub, enjoying a delightfully unhealthy fare washed down with home brewed beer and not doing a very good job of keeping their "relationship" a secret. He would take her hand, put her pinky into his mouth and run his tongue around it. She would giggle and pull her hand back, but would run her bare foot up his leg under the table.

As she opened up her mouth preparing to take in a french fry he was holding out to her, she heard a familiar accented voice coming from the TV. She looked up and sure enough, it was Marla in all her glory on Lou Dobbs.

"Well hot damn! It's her"

"Huh?"

"It's her!" her voice somewhat raised, "it's the whore that took my husband"

Jake turned around and looked at the TV.

"Oh...wow! Well, at least she's hot! Imagine how you would have felt if she was not as good looking as you" he laughed but Beth was not amused.

"If that is supposed to be compliment to *me*, it didn't sound like one and if it was supposed to be a joke, it didn't sound like that either. Does every man have to worship at this woman's throne?"

"I hardly think I am worshipping her, Beth, take it easy! She's just on TV, she can't hurt you here"

"Yeah? Well, she *is* hurting me, and I want to leave!"

"We only just got our food"

"Well, you eat it then..." she threw back at him and stormed toward the exit.

He signaled for the waiter to pack up the food to go "I'll come back for it in a minute," he ran out after her.

"Beth" he said gently trying to embrace her from behind.

"I am a little angry right now, Jake" she pulled away from him.

"It's a tough thing to get over and it's still kind of fresh for you. I shouldn't have joked like that, I'm sorry..."

She was pleased with his apology but she remained turned away from him, standing with her arms folded in front of her.

"...but Beth," he went on, "I'm no good at lying. I say it the way I see it. This might sound harsh, but you need to let this shit go!"

"Oh, here we go again" she attempted to walk away.

"No, listen to me" he grabbed her and held her fast "You cannot keep running from this. It's not going to go away. It's always going to be there because it happened! You are a beautiful woman. She is a beautiful woman too. So your husband has good taste. We don't know if he was planning to leave you for her or if it was just something that happened..."

"People don't just *happen* to have sex, Jake...they intend it...just like I did with you"

"It's true we act on desire, but it's not always planned. Sometimes it happens like hot spontaneity. Like it *could* have happened for us, if *you* had not stood in the way with all your *planning.* Look, I am not saying it was right, okay? Maybe it just happened or maybe he had some kinda reason"

"So it's all my fault again"

"I didn't say that. What I mean is that you will never know what really happened or how to deal with it if you don't face it! You need to face him. It might help you get over it or at least decide how to move forward."

She stared at him angrily, "What the hell do you know, Jake?"

"I know enough to know that when shit happens, it does not always mean the end. Sometimes it means a brand new beginning." He moved toward her, taking her hand. She did not resist. "I also know that I really like you and it bugs the hell out of me to see you get so hot and bothered every time this comes up. Shit, if I had my way you'd just forget all about him and hang out with me."

He turned her around and pulled her into his arms. His breath felt warm behind her ears as he whispered, "But I am not blind…I know you love him. So I'll take what I can get…" a gentle kiss behind her ear, "…while I can." A gentle kiss on the nape of her neck, "Wanna go home?"

"Jake, you are too damn much. What am I supposed to do with you?"

"Take me home and make mad passionate love to me?"

She laughed heartily, all her anger diffused. "You are right, about everything. I guess I do have to deal with it…"

"Ok, but not right now…I'm going in to get our food. Be right back"

She stood staring at a large potted plant thinking about what Jake had said. He really was right. She did still love Cal. That's why it still hurt. It did have to be dealt with. But how? And when? Now? Now, when she was feeling more sensual and sexual and beautiful than she had in years? Now, when she was discovering new highs in her sexuality? Now, when she was enjoying this young interesting smart man's undivided attention? She was just as bad as Cal! Is this how he had felt with Marla?

She sensed anger rising and decided not to go there. Spinning around rapidly in hopes of erasing all thoughts of Cal and Marla, she almost bumped into a tall lady wearing a big wide brimmed summer hat who was walking by.

"I am so sorry" she fumbled.

"It's okay" The lady responded in a husky voice. Something about it seemed familiar. She tried to catch a glance at the lady's face under her hat and behind the large sunglasses she wore, but it was difficult and she was about to give up when the lady reached up to take off her sunglasses and said, "Bethany?"

"Oh my God! Sister Sophie???"

"Oh, please drop the Sister, we are not in church here"

Sister Sophie was the daughter of Pastor Rivers, head pastor at Blessed Jordan Evangelical Church where Beth and Cal attended. Sister Sophie and her husband Burt ran the marriage and family counselling ministry there and they led by example. When Pastor Burt gave the sermon, Sister Sophie would sit on her throne-like chair on the stage and watch lovingly as he preached the Word with youthful vigor and eloquence. He certainly had a gift and it was common knowledge that Pastor Rivers was preparing to leave the church to his son-in-law whenever he chose to retire, which would not be soon since Pastor Rivers seemed to be getting better with age. His sermons went deeper and touched you in places you hadn't looked in a while. His wisdom grew with age and experience and Bible study sessions were always packed as people just wanted to be able to hear him give his wise counsel in a more intimate setting.

God did not spare on looks when He created the Rivers family either and Sister Sophie inherited much of her father's grace and elegance. Tall and slender, smooth ebony skin, a perfectly molded face and eyes that sparkled out at you all the way from the pulpit.

Now here she stood, still tall, but very skinny. Her eyes still sparkled and apart from the drastic weight loss, she seemed to look the same, but something was off.

"What are you doing here?" Beth blurted out in embarrassment.

"I live here now"

"You do? I am surprised I have not bumped into you before"

"Why, how long have you been here?"

"A few weeks, and I come into town just about every day"

"Well, I am not always out and about alone. This is a rare and pleasurable moment. And whenever Burt comes to take me out, we usually drive out to one of the neighboring towns."

"I am so sorry Sister Sophie…I mean, Sophie, but I am so confused…and it's none of my business, so forgive me for asking, but why did you move so far from home?"

"Ha! Long story! I'll tell you one day. Why don't you come over some time? I still take visitors. I am on Collins Street. Third house on the left."

"Er…I…Sure," The invitation caught Beth unawares. Sophie had always been nice to her in a distant sort of way, so a casual invitation to her home felt strange, "…I'd like that" she lied.

Just then Jake came up behind them with the doggy bags, "Hi!"

"Oh! Hi!" Beth's discomfort took an exponential jump. She had hoped Sister Sophie would be gone before Jake came back. "Er… Sophie, this is Jake…my…er…gardener. He's really good if you need one."

Sister Sophie smiled sweetly as she shook his hand, "Oh, nice to meet you. I don't have much of a garden, just a lawn and a few pots. That's nature enough for me."

"That's cool! So Beth, you do know someone round here after all?"

"I had no idea"

"Anyway, I better get moving on. Really nice seeing you, Beth. Don't be too shy to come by. I am just regular here and I am alone. Nice to meet you, Jake. Bye!"

They stood looking after her for a few minutes.

"You alright? You look a little out of it. Or are you just feeling *busted*?" he laughed.

"I dunno how I feel right now. That was kind of weird. I like her, but she has never said more than was necessary to me in church and yet here she is inviting me over; and she is living all the way out here and her husband *comes to take her out* as she put it and well…there is just something different about her, but I can't put my finger on it. It's just weird!"

"Let's just go home"

"Sounds good to me!"

13

She lay in his arms awake. She didn't want to move in case she woke him up. She just wanted to lay there and enjoy the moment. She knew this relationship could go nowhere, but she was enjoying it so much as it was. Maybe it was the sex, maybe it was his young strong body, maybe it was his mind, or maybe it was just a welcome distraction. She looked at his peaceful sleeping face.

It was definitely all of the above, she smiled.

How could she ever condemn Cal now, when she was in some ways worse? At least Marla was an older woman…Jake was just…a child. A child in a man's body, with an extremely mature mind. Jake was anything but typical. She let out a sigh and he moved.

She smiled at him as he opened his eyes, "Good morning, Lover"

He smiled in return, "I like that"

She kissed him and he pulled her close and began to kiss her ardently as he pushed his morning excitement against her thighs.

She moaned and moved under him so that he was where he needed to be.

But before he went further he stopped and gazed at her face intently.

"What's the matter?" she asked.

"This is such a dangerous game we are playing, Ms. Lambeau" he said stroking her short hair.

"I really *really* like you, I really enjoy being with you and I really REALLY love having sex with you. You are like no other woman I have ever met."

"Mmm…so what's so dangerous about that, Mr. Blumenthal?" she said running her fingers through his hair in return.

"I could really fall in love with you"

"Shhhh" she put a finger to his lips. "We agreed not to use the L word. This is fun, let's just enjoy it."

"Yeah…I know" he said and he pushed himself inside her.

They had bathed and eaten and were just being lazy when they heard a sound from downstairs.

"Does anyone else have a key" he asked

"Only my mother" she replied. "I'd better go see" she stood up and put on a robe, covering her lacy lounge wear.

"I'll be right behind you. If anyone is here to hurt you, I'm killing them"

She smiled, "My hero" she whispered and leaned over to give him a kiss.

"Mom?" Winston stood in the doorway. They had not heard him come up the stairs.

"Stoney? What the…"

"Don't stop on my account. I'll just leave"

"No, Stoney, wait!"

She ran down the stairs after him, Jake right behind her, wearing boxers.

Stoney had already made it to the front door.

"Stoney!"

He turned to look at her. She tightened her robe around herself.

"Stoney, I'm sorry. I just never expected anyone to come out here"

"That's obvious!"

"I…I don't know what to say…I…" she stammered.

"So this…" he indicated Jake with a look of intense disdain etched on his face, "…is the midlife crisis Dad thinks you are going through? This is the reason you left Dad?"

"What?"

"He is at home pining over you and you are whoring yourself away out here."

"Stoney!" She was in shock, he had never cursed at her before.

Jake had stepped forward, "Hey! Show your mother some respect!"

"And why don't you go fuck someone your own age… Motherfucker…literally."

"And why don't you ask your father who the real whore is?!"

"You gonna bring my Dad into this?"

"Well, did he tell you that he was the one fucking someone else?"

"Mention my Dad one more time asshole"

"He's a fucking coward. Lying to his son"

Winston rushed at Jake, they fell against the table and rolled onto the floor.

Beth finally came out of her shock and to her senses, screaming for them to stop fighting.

She tried to tear them apart and got thrown against the wall.

"Stop it," she screamed. "Please! Just stop it!"

"Apologize to her" Jake was saying when Winston threw him an unexpected punch to the face.

"Fuck you!"

Jake got one back at him straight into the belly

"Ugh" Winston grunted rolling off him holding on to his midsection.

Jake took the opportunity and jumped on him, holding him down,

"Apologize!"

"Let me go!"

"Please Jake get off of him, let him go!" Beth shouted.

"He needs to learn some respect"

"Let him go!" she insisted.

He got off Winston and stood back.

Winston stood up, glared at his mother and Jake in turn, picked up his bag and walked out.

Jake, breathing hard, let himself down on the floor beside Beth and reached an arm around her as she knelt on the floor crying.

"Leave me alone" she sobbed through her tears.

"Hey, I was the one defending your honor here."

"Just go please! Just get your shit and get out!"

"That's the man you're crying over? Couldn't even tell his own son the truth about what he did. What kind of bullshit is that? and you are sending *me* away???"

"Go!!!" she yelled, looking him dead in the face.

He backed up in disbelief, turned around and hurried up the stairs, cursing all the way.

She remained on the floor sobbing and was still there when he came back down with his clothes on, heading to the door.

"You know, you are not the first older woman I have been with. I never lied to make it seem like you were. But I gotta tell you Beth, you are by far the most complicated. I am so fucking over this shit. I hope you figure yourself out… for your own sake. Cos I don't give a fuck! And in case you think you can call out to me when you are passing by sometime…well, don't!"

He was gone!

She let herself fall into a fetal position and sobbed.

A shower and a glass of wine later, she worked around the house tidying up the mess that the boys' scuffle had left.

As she cleaned, she was quiet and in her thoughts. She was resigned to her fate, whatever it was. Her husband had kept his secret from his son, making him look like the angel while she was now the demon and whore. Nice!

She could not be mad at anyone, since she had not kept in touch with anyone for the last few weeks. Maybe her mother would have warned her that Stoney was coming, had she kept her phone on or at least checked her messages. There was no one to blame for this but herself. It seemed that since discovering Cal's affair, every action she took was the wrong one.

So she was resigned. Whatever will be will be. The one thing that was clear, was that it was time to start facing the situation. Just as Jake…poor Jake…Just as Jake had said that day outside the Pub when she had bumped into…Ah yes!…That was it! Sister Sophie!

Beth stood in front of the third house on Collins Street. It was a beautiful white colonial home. The yard was exactly as Sister Sophie had described, just a well-kept lawn. The big porch had a few flower pots and a large swing. It looked welcoming enough, albeit very quiet.

Beth walked up the paved pathway, up the porch steps and rang the doorbell.

There were some sounds to be heard from inside and the door was opened to her by a young lady she did not recognize.

"Hello" the lady said with a quizzical smile, "may I help you?"

"Um, yes, I am here to see Sister Sophie, I am not sure if I have the right house."

"Oh yes, yes, you do. Come on in, your timing is pretty good, she just woke up. Whom shall I tell her is here."

"Bethany Lambeau"

"Right this way, Ms. Lambeau"

Beth was led into a beautiful living room furnished with white cane furniture. The shag area rug at the center of the room was apple green and lay on a perfectly polished White Oak hardwood floor. The white walls were ordained with large oil paintings of florals in pastel shades and leafy plants in medium to light shades of green. Sheer white curtains hung lightly around the large French windows which stood open, overlooking the manicured lawn. With the sun streaming in from almost every side, it gave a feeling of being in a gazebo. It felt airy, sunny and free.

"This is my favorite room in the house! Welcome! I am so glad you came to visit."

Beth turned around to see Sister Sophie walking in dressed in casual slacks with a flowing silk blouse and though she maintained her height, her easy elegance and her beautifully flawless skin covering her perfectly chiseled cheekbones, Beth was almost certain that she looked even skinnier than the last time she had seen her.

"Lissette, please bring us some iced lemonade."

14

"Sit down!" Sister Sophie beckoned for Beth to have a seat close to her on one of the cane two-seaters, "Apart from Lissette, I don't get much female company my age. This is going to be fun"

Though she did not look like she was lying, her words seemed to be more enthusiastic than her tone of voice or mannerisms. Beth didn't know quite how to take all this. She didn't understand what Sister Sophie was talking about. Why was no one coming to visit? Why was she here?

Beth began to question why she herself was here but knowing it was too late to back out, she just smiled.

"It *is* a really nice house" she managed to feign.

Sister Sophie launched into an elaborate history of the house, stopping only to allow Lissette to pour the lemonade from the crystal pitcher into their glasses.

When she was done, Beth sat in silence wringing her hands, not sure what to say.

"So what's the matter, Beth? You wanna talk about it?"

"What's that?"

"Oh come on, I've been doing this too long. I can tell you need to talk. What is it?"

Bethany wondered if therapists and counsellors were born with voices like this or if it was something that was taught, because Sophie's deep voice seemed to have dropped to that perfect gentle motherly pitch that brought all your secrets out of you.

"Er…well, I guess I am feeling guilty. Actually, I am not sure what I am feeling, I am all conflicted. Nothing is making sense right now and I feel like it's all my fault and I can't begin to think of how to fix it."

"Maybe you're not meant to fix it."

"I don't even know if I really want it fixed."

"Hmm, well, that's interesting. So what is it exactly? Apart from maybe that cutie you were with the other day."

"Was it that obvious?"

"Were you trying to hide it?" she laughed. "He *is* a good reason to feel guilty, isn't he?"

Beth let out a giggle, "that's funny, but…it's over"

"What happened?"

"My son walked in unexpectedly"

"Oh, Shoot! That calls for something stronger than lemonade… Lissette can mix a mean drink, want one?"

"Sister Sophie!!!"

"Look, first of all, we ain't in church here, so drop the sister stuff and secondly you do not have to pretend or be on your best behavior here. Just be real, girl. You're not saying anything I haven't heard before and quite honestly, sometimes a drink is just what's needed. So do you want one? It's up to you."

"No thanks, really, I'm good…at least for now."

"Okay, so tell me the whole thing, start from the beginning."

Beth took a deep breath and began the whole story from the party at Marla's apartment. Sophie was a great listener, probably another thing they taught in counselling school, she never took her eyes off Beth and she cooed and hmmed, nodded and shook her head at all the right places. She listened with complete non-judgment.

"…and now here I am. Even more confused than before. I know I should have just stayed there and talked it out and worked it out with him, I know that would have been the right thing to do…"

"Says who?"

"Well, isn't it?"

"Well, is it?"

"I don't understand"

"What makes it the right thing?"

"Everybody knows it's the right thing to do…you are not supposed to walk out on him, you certainly are not supposed to replace him even if it's temporary. Two wrongs don't make a right. How are we ever supposed to get back together now?"

"So is that what you want?"

"What? No. I mean maybe, I mean I don't know. I…I just don't know"

Sister Sophie remained silent.

"…and you are not helping"

"Why?"

"You are not saying anything! That's why. You are supposed to tell me what to do. Isn't that your job? You just said you've been doing this so long, I am not saying anything you haven't heard before, so go on! You must have a ready answer for me"

Sister Sophie totally ignored her outburst, "I do have a question though"

"What?"

"How do you feel?"

"How do I feel??? Seriously??? I am getting angry right now. That's how I feel"

"Because I am not telling you what to do? Or what you want to hear?"

"Something!!!! Yes!!"

"Have you asked Bethany?"

"What???"

"Seems like you are looking for answers everywhere. But you only need to look in one place. Here!..." she pointed at Beth's heart, "It doesn't matter what I think, or what your Mom says, or what Jake says, or what Stoney may think of you or even what Cal wants. What matters is what makes sense to you. What is right for you. Making choices based on anyone else's opinions only leads to unhappiness"

"What about...you know...God?"

"Be still! And know that I am God – Psalm 46 Verse 10. If you listen, He will speak. He is right there." A pause. A deep breath. "And now you'll forgive me if smoke"

"Wha? I...er...I guess I...er..."

"You are too cute Beth" Sophie laughed as she pulled a wooden box out of a drawer in the side table next to her. "Shocked, are you? Pastor's daughter smoking!! Whoa!!! You just always believe the picture that's painted, don't you?"

"Yes...I guess I do"

"But the picture is always just that...a picture! An interpretation by the artist of the truth. And one artist's interpretation is not another's, just as one artist's truth, is not another's'"

"But there is only one Truth, isn't there?"

"Well, yes, I do believe that there is the One Truth from which all things rise, but outside of that...it's all interpretation" She lit her joint and took a drag.

"Sister Sophie...you are barely short of blaspheming here"

Sister Sophie threw her head back in laughter, "It's medical marijuana – I need it for the discomfort, sometimes it's pain, and I need it for the fear."

"I'm sorry?"

"Oh, you must not know? I'm dying"

"You are what?"

She took a drag of her joint, held it and then slowly let it out,

"I have inoperable metastatic breast cancer. I am told I am on my last leg. That's why I am out here. I didn't want to spend my last days being my Dad's perfect daughter. I wanted to spend this time really drawing close to the One who is calling me back. Not through service, but through solitude and meditation."

In a flash everything at last made sense to Beth. Why Sophie had lost so much weight, why she was here alone, why she wasn't getting visitors her age, why Sister Toni and the others were in town that other day. Beth shook her head in disbelief,

"But...but it can't be. Are you sure? How can this happen? I just can't believe this"

"I know! It's always hard when you first hear it. But you get used to the idea and submit yourself to it soon enough. And I must confess, once you surrender, it's not all that bad. Except for those moments of fear. And that's when you light up a joint," She took another drag and smiled, "works wonders! Was Burt's idea. Smart man, my Burt"

"I don't know what to say. I am here lamenting about my ridiculous problems and you are sitting there facing death so calmly. I am being so selfish"

"Oh, spare me, Beth! You may enjoy your self-flagellation, but please don't do it at my expense. And trust me, I am nowhere near calm about facing death."

For a moment both women sat in silence. Sophie spoke first, staring out in front of her,

"One thing staring death in the face does, is make you more honest. I guess 'cos you don't want to die in a lie or you just don't give a fuck any more about what people think. I mean why should I care? They are the ones who'll have to deal with it after I am gone." She chuckled to herself then looked up at Beth. "I'm sorry."

"It's no problem. I think I understand."

"You are right...you only *think* you do, but you can't understand". Her straight stare made Beth feel unsettled.

"No...I can't," she muttered tearing her eyes away awkwardly.

"I am sorry, Beth, I am feeling rather tired. I absolutely need to take a rest."

Beth jumped up, "Of course, of course. I am so sorry"

Sister Sophie rolled her eyes as she stood up supporting herself on the arm rest,

"Would you stop being so sorry all the time! Stop apologizing! Stop trying so hard. Just BE. You are already perfect!..."

Beth had to bite her tongue to avoid saying that she was so sorry again.

"...getting on my nerves with that stuff!" Sophie continued as Lissette came to her assistance helping her into the hall.

"You know what?" Sophie stopped and looked back at Beth with a huge smile on her face.

"Tomorrow I will come to your place! You can draw me."

"Er, Sophie, you are welcome to come over, but I have not drawn people in a long time. I do more abstract work these days."

"Okay, draw me in abstract! I'm serious"

"Putting me on the spot"

"Best place to be, Beth, best place to be" she turned and Lissette helped her beyond the staircase.

Minutes later, Lissette saw Beth to the door.

"Er...is it true? Her condition?" she had to ask. Lissette nodded gravely. "How long?"

"Whatever time God gives her, she has lasted longer than they gave her already. It's day by day."

"Oh, my God!" Beth felt herself shaking with emotion.

Lissette touched her shoulder in comfort, "She really enjoyed your company. Perhaps you have found your purpose for being in Dunham. See you tomorrow?"

"Yes...yes of course. Thank you. Does she need anything?"

Lissette shook her head and smiled, "Just you."

15

The blackness of night engulfed The Farm. All the beauty of the newly created garden was hidden behind the dark veil thick with silence pierced only by the sound of crickets and a far off owl.

Bethany's bed stood empty but for the rumpled sheets. The rest of the house stood shadowy but for a single standing lamp directly behind Bethany as she sat in front of a small canvas quietly and intently painting thick and heavy strokes leaving no canvas uncovered. Already there was a completed piece on the floor drying. Completing the second piece, she placed it beside the first to dry, picked up a third canvas and began again.

She had tossed and turned, unable to sleep. Too many thoughts running through her mind. Sophie, the young and beautiful daughter of a most charismatic pastor, was dying. Far away from her husband and family. Alone. What sense did that make? What sense did it make that she was dying? Was there no way of saving her? There were so many things one could try these days. Surely there was something out there for her. Sophie was Beth's age. What if this happened to *her*? Wait a minute, how long had it been since her last mammogram? Or what if it were not breast cancer but something else that would claim her life? What would become of Stoney? And Cal…

She got up and went downstairs to paint.

॰ॶ

It was late afternoon when the cobalt blue BMW pulled up outside The Farm.

Lissette helped Sister Sophie into the house and Bethany noticed how weak and frail she was looking. Was this the first time she noticed it? Or was it just that much more pronounced today? She wasn't sure which it was, but she made every effort to remain positive and lively, offering juice and fruit.

Sophie waved off every offer, demanding to be seated in the love seat Beth had specially prepared for her and after she was settled, she ordered Lissette on an errand.

Lissette could not have been more hesitant to leave, protesting as much as she could. But Sophie was adamant.

"I don't care if I had a rough morning, Lissette! The worst thing that could happen here is that I keel over and stop breathing."

"Er...that's kind of bad, I think," said Beth trying to insert some humor.

"Oh, she watches me like a hawk," continued Sophie angrily. "It's gonna happen sometime with or without you, Lissette. I want to be alone here for a while. Please just go!"

Beth didn't know what to do. She looked from one to the other, trying to decide what the right thing to say or do would be. Lissette saved her.

"Ok. I'll go. I'll give you a couple of hours, ok? Then I am coming back, ok?" Sophie ignored her, staring instead at Beth's newest paintings.

Lissette gave Beth her number to call in case of emergency, but when Beth nervously asked her exactly what the emergency might entail, Lissette only said, "Just call me, I won't be far away"

Shutting the door behind Lissette, Beth turned to see Sophie totally engrossed in her night's work.

"What are these?" Sophie asked.

"I just did those last night" She said feigning a calm attitude as she headed over to her easel and began to prepare some pencils, "I couldn't sleep. So I came down to paint."

"I like them"

"That's good, since you sort of inspired them"

"Me? Really?" Sophie forced a laugh. "You couldn't sleep because of me?"

"Well, I am still digesting this whole... this thing..." she gestured at Sophie as she came toward her and began to arrange her dress and position for the portrait, "...and I...well, I was thinking about our mortality last night. Yours, mine, all of us. I mean just because I am not obviously sick, does not make my death any less imminent than yours...I'm sorry...I didn't mean it like that..."

"It's ok! I think about it every day" Sophie said quietly as she allowed herself to be positioned. "Every day for the last ten years."

A heavy silence fell between them. Beth stood back looking at her model and satisfied with the pose, headed back to the easel and sat on her stool.

Sophie remained silent, staring off into space.

"So..." Beth began sheepishly, "...why was it a rough morning for you today?"

Sophie shrugged in response turning away, "I have good days and bad days....The space between them is getting steadily shorter..."

Beth felt so guilty and stupid that she had asked the question. She was at a loss trying to figure out what to say to rectify the situation as the silence grew palpably heavier.

Then Sophie went on, "...I keep my spirits up for everyone...most times it's real...but sometimes I have to pretend. Now,...I am getting weaker...And it's getting harder..."

She looked up at Beth, her eyes pleading and Beth answered the call without hesitation, rushing to Sophie's side on the two seater, putting her arms around her and holding her close. No words were needed, which was good since she had none. She just held her and Sophie surrendered.

"I thought I had it beat," she whispered through the developing sobs, tears welling up in her eyes. "I thought I was one of the lucky ones. Huh! But why? Why would *I* ever be one of the lucky ones?...

...But I *am* lucky, right? I get to leave this shit early and get to experience warm and eternal Love on the other side. No more struggles. No more lies. But then...then why was I here at all? What was the point of it all? What am I leaving behind? I'll be gone soon, and it will be like I was never even here. Why was I here? Why did I even bother? What was the point, Beth? What was the point of it all?...

...So I am holding on as long as I can...but...I can't...I can't hold on anymore. I'm slipping...I'm losing..."

Sophie wept.

Sophie's head lay on Beth's lap. Beth, her dress wet with Sophie's tears, sat stroking Sophie's thinning hair, as they both stared out in front of them.

"Epiphany" said Sophie.

"Sorry?"

"That's what those paintings should be called, 'Epiphany'"

"Epiphany" Beth repeated and smiled. "Yes! I like it!"

"I think I am going to like my portrait."

"I think we should get started on it so that you actually have one"

Sophie laughed, "Yes, you are right, maybe we should get started." She sat up.

"Let me bring you a washcloth to clean up."

"No, don't. Let it be real. The real me as I am right now. And in fact...do you mind if I smoke?"

"Mi casa es su casa, Sophie. You can do anything you want here"

Sophie laughed and lit up and Beth was relieved to see her coming back to herself again.

"Draw me as I am…" she took a drag of her joint and exhaled slowly, "…Smokin'!"

Lissette had come back with a light take out dinner and having satisfied herself that Sophie was ok, she had agreed to leave Sophie there longer and to return only when called.

And so the ladies sat and chatted and laughed like teenagers, while Beth moved around with a sketch pad drawing sketches of Sophie from different angles and in different positions. She mentioned that she would later turn the sketches into paintings and Sophie thought the idea delightful. "You could do a whole show about me in my last days and call it *Epiphany – Answering the Call*" she enthused, as she happily positioned and repositioned herself as needed.

On her own, Beth would not have had the courage even to think of this idea, let alone find it acceptable, but with Sophie's force behind her, she actually felt inspired.

"So what's the story with you and Burt?" Beth wanted to know, "How is he ok with you being so far away and so sick?"

"Oh, that's *my* choice, poor sweetheart. He'd be here in a minute, if I let him. He wanted me to stay at home but I wasn't having it. I didn't want to be there with the whole church fussing over me and he can't be here because the church needs him. Daddy needs him."

"Aren't you worried that the people will say he is abandoning you in your hour of need?"

"Beth, I could care less what the people say. Daddy and Burt will have to figure that one out for themselves. What to say and how to deal with it. This is *their* dream, not mine. I pulled out of church admin seven months ago. The leadership knows as much as they need to and they come by to pray and all that good stuff. But me and

Burt's personal business is gonna stay just that - our personal business. Besides, we already have a replacement plan in place. So we are good."

"A replacement plan?"

She nodded, "Oh yeah, I set Burt free a long time ago."

"What do you mean, you set him free?"

"I mean that our relationship is not dictated by possession, control or jealousy. We made an agreement very early on and it stuck. He had his and I had mine."

"You...you mean other people? You were unfaithful to each other? Both of you?"

"We were never *unfaithful*. There are zero secrets between us. Complete honesty. Not easy. Sometimes very hurtful, but an open relationship was the only way it could work for us in our situation. We are first and foremost best friends"

Beth stared at Sophie in disbelief and confusion.

"Burt and I already knew each other from church circles before we met again in Bible school. He was answering 'The Call', I was doing what was expected of me. We hung out a lot and it was obvious that he was getting feelings for me, but he never pushed it and everything was fine until I fell in love...only not with him. I fell for this waitress at an off campus diner we often went to. She was beautiful. She had the most amazing legs that went on forever, but she had a flat butt," Sophie giggled, "I always teased her about that. Her laugh was contagious and she was courageous and bold and loud. She was everything I wished I could be."

Sophie looked up and smirked when she saw the shock on Beth's face.

"Yes! A woman! I knew then that I could never live up to my father's expectations of me. Knew that I would never be the perfect pastor's daughter. I felt like a failure. And the only one I could talk to about it was Burt. And you know what he did when I told him?" Beth shook her head. "He asked me to marry him. He said he would love me enough for both of us. He would protect me. Protect my secret.

All he wanted was to be with me. Romantic, isn't it? He meant it too. Every word. But my Burt had his own ambitions too. Yes, he would have me, *and* the church. He'd be the perfect son to my father, which he is, and he would take over the church someday, which he will. Everyone gets what they want. Everybody is happy."

Beth was trying to keep a passive look on her face without success. She was completely shocked at these revelations. Sophie went on,

"I am not sure what I thought my future would look like, but he made so much sense to me and he was so sweet and kind. He loved me so much and I knew I truly loved him too. I said yes and that night was the first time we made love. Maybe he was hoping it would win me over completely. Maybe he always thought that he would one day. But for me I just had to be sure that it could work for us physically. After all, this is the rest of our lives we were talking about."

"And I guess it worked?" said Beth.

"Yes, it worked. It worked very well. And so my lie began. Me, Burt and my family on one side, me and Phoebe on the other.

We had a good two years before I was busted and it got round to Daddy. He was furious. Went on about how I was a disgrace to the church and to God and the family name, and that I was destroying all that he had worked for. I tried to play it off as a one-time experiment, but I think he knew. I think he'd always known. That I didn't want to run the church, that I was a closet lesbian, that I was a misfit. He knew! He just pretended not to.

When I tried to call Phoebe after that, she never returned my calls. I think Daddy might have sent someone over to scare her or pay her off. I never saw her again. And it hurt like hell. She was the love of my life. She was the one that got away.

And Burt, he stood by me, but I think this brought it home for him and he realized then that he could never have all of me. It was after this that he began to see others. God knows there were enough opportunities. I always wondered if Daddy knew. I'll bet he did, but things are different for men you see. I am almost certain that Daddy had his own moments too. Women literally throw themselves at the Pastor.

So things opened up for Burt, but shut down for me. I just conditioned myself to become the person I was expected to be. And then two blows in one year – I couldn't have children and I had breast cancer.

I was sure I was being punished for being what I was so, when I went into remission, I welcomed it as a second chance to get it right. I became the part. Embodied the role. I died to myself trying to redeem myself. I surrendered all and then ten years later, boom! It's baaack. And this time, without an escape clause. But it's all good, because now Daddy's perfect son-in-law will marry the perfect church girl we have chosen for him and they will all run the perfect church. No more disappointments!"

"Except maybe that your father is losing his daughter…his flesh and blood"

"Phh! I don't think that matters much to him. The church, the church…it's always been about the church. He has literally adopted Burt as his own, and Burt will bring him the glory he dreamed of. That's my one redeeming contribution, I brought Burt into the mix."

"Oh Sophie, I am so sure you are wrong."

Sophie looked at Beth, "You are cute, you know that? I have lived with him all my life, Beth. Don't you think I know the man? He is a Bible believing man of God and I am an abomination in his eyes"

"Yes, but you are his daughter! I know what it's like to be a parent. I know that no matter how much my son defies my dreams for him, I could never love him less."

"I didn't say that he doesn't love me but he cannot reconcile his love with what the Lord abhors and I make it easier for him not to have to, by keeping myself quiet and out of sight as much as possible. I don't want to hurt him, Beth! I can see it in his eyes when he looks at me. I know what he is thinking"

"Have you asked him? Has he ever told you how he feels?"

"Oh come on!!! Ok, fine, tell me this…if he loves me so much, where is he? Huh? Why doesn't he come here to see me? Not once in the months since I've moved out here. Not once!"

"I…" Beth was at a loss, "…I'm sorry"

"Yeah…so am I!…But it's all good. I am at peace with it all. He has to be the man God made him to be. He is an amazing preacher, a great leader, a pastor who genuinely cares and loves his people. He is a true example of a man who has found his purpose and is living it to the fullest. Somewhere in God's own mind, there is a reason why I came to be this man's daughter. I haven't quite figured it out yet, but I am in awe of him and all that he stands for. And I am completely at peace with his choices concerning me. It's just the way it's meant to be. Everything is exactly the way it's meant to be. You have to accept it and learn to love it. That is surrender. It's a big lesson. It might be what I was here to learn."

Much as she tried, Beth could not hide her look of incredulity.

"Honestly Beth, don't worry about me. I am at peace!"

How could she argue with that?

16

Beth breathed in the crisp morning air as she jogged through the now familiar streets of Dunham, musing upon how all semblance of her former life seemed to have vanished along with all semblance of her former self. Just a few weeks ago she had felt broken, without purpose and alone and now, thanks to Sophie, she was filled with intention and inspiration. She woke every morning excited and ended every night with eager expectation for the next day. There was no fixed plan or rigid routine to her days. Most of her time was spent with Sophie, as they philosophized, laughed and cried, danced and sang together as if they had known each other for several lifetimes.

Every conversation with Sophie gave Beth more fodder for contemplation. Sophie was nothing if not intriguing. She could speak about things that obviously hurt her deeply with ease and detachment. And through everything, she continued to focus on love. There was no question about it, this woman was an Angel.

It could not be said that being with Sophie made her think less about Cal. On the contrary, much of their conversation, without being forced, spoke about him. Who he was, who she was, who they were together. In turn, Sophie spoke about her life with Burt who, though not there physically, was always very present. Beth watched as Sophie spoke to him on the phone and was warmed by the palpable love and friendship between them.

"How can it work this way between you two" she asked curious, "how can you be so close when there is someone else?"

"I guess it's a matter of both of us knowing that this is the way it is and accepting it" Sophie shrugged. "She is a lovely girl and I know he is happy with her. But I know he is happy with me too. Each relationship is special in its own way. There are things that are just for us and there are things that are just for them. He tells me everything, not sure he does the same with her. But I am sure somewhere inside herself, she is just waiting for the day that she will have him to herself. Patience. That is the difference between this and most other open relationships…this one has a definite expected end"

No matter how Sophie sliced it, this open relationship idea was one that Beth would never be able to consider. And that was the beauty of their freedom of sharing; it was not about her taking on a life like Sophie's. It was about accepting each other exactly as they were, for exactly who they were. It gave Beth such a relief to be able to feel completely free and unashamed of who she was, and what she felt. This freedom seemed to provide her with the space to begin to understand and accept herself exactly as she was accepting Sophie. With her acceptance, she began to feel compassion for herself. With compassion came forgiveness. And with forgiveness came love. Slowly but surely, she was dropping her negativity about herself. Looking in the mirror, she did not feel sorry, anger or despair. She felt good. She no longer saw only the flaws of the woman that looked back at her. In fact, she began to like who she saw.

"What about…well, you know…women. I mean, don't you miss…you know?"

Sophie laughed at Beth's awkwardness. "Yes, Beth, if I am to be honest, I do miss being with a woman. A woman's touch, her feel, her kiss. But I had to give that up. What good would it do getting into a relationship destined for destruction? Everyone gets hurt. I have had 'special' friends, but eventually I accepted that the closet would have to be a cozy home for me. Maybe if I didn't get sick, I would have built up enough courage to one day come out and stand up for good Christian girls that love girls." she laughed. "That might have been a fun and fearful thing to do."

"Would you have gone looking for Phoebe?"

Sophie gave it some thought, then slowly shook her head.

"No, that was years ago. No use. I do wonder what happened to her. Where did she go in life? Who did she end up with? At least she would never be living a lie."

"Maybe you can still come out and make a stand?"

"That's why I love you, Beth. You are so funny"

"But I mean it. I mean what can happen now? You said yourself that your father knows already. You are no longer active in the Church leadership, so why not?"

"I just…I can't. I just can't and I won't. The end!"

Sophie's one sore spot was her love for her father who so clearly held his distance from her.

Beth's heart went out to her. If only she could help her mend that one real fracture that had never healed. The subject was a no go area. Sophie could become extremely obstinate and stubborn when it came to this. And there was no moving her.

As different as they were, their comfort in each other's presence and the bond forming between them was undeniable.

"Why didn't we become friends sooner?" Beth asked once as they sat at the window of Sophie's living room watching the smoke from her lips curl and disappear into the night sky.

"Because we weren't ready yet" Sophie had an answer for everything.

"I just don't want it to be too late" Beth sighed.

"No, this is the perfect time and place. Everything is exactly the way it is meant to be. And isn't it wonderful?"

Beth really wanted to say 'yes and I wish it would never end' but instead she said, "Yes it is and I am very happy."

"Atta girl!" Sophie smiled.

The Farm had been turned into a true workshop dedicated to the Epiphany Collection.

The living room walls were covered with photos of Sophie that Beth had printed out at the local copy shop. Between the photos there were rough sketches as Beth responded to every burst of inspiration.

Along one wall there was an array of incomplete paintings. Some barely begun, some just requiring finishing touches.

Sophie was everywhere – asleep, in pain, smoking, laughing, deep in thought, every way that Beth could capture her. While the subject remained the same, Beth was creative with the backgrounds, matching them with Sophie's moods. In this way she was able to enjoy the freedom of experimenting and incorporating different artistic styles. Work became play and she was having a great time with it.

She felt especially good this morning because she had finally finished the first portrait. Her first ever commissioned piece of work. She felt confident but was still nervous about showing it. Nonetheless, knowing that Sophie had been fervently looking forward to this, she could barely wait for her to come and see it, so she took her run by Sophie's home to invite her over for a look.

She arrived at the house excited but as she approached the front door, she noticed a bright yellow sticky note addressed to her.

She grabbed it as she felt her heart sink.

"We are at the hospital" Lissette had written, giving the address.

Beth felt a pain in her chest and was not sure if she was breathing at all. She suddenly felt faint and held on to the door post to compose herself.

Heading down the street, she prayed as she walked, becoming more and more overcome with emotion with each step until she had to stop and hold on to a fence. She leaned over and cried begging "God Please. Please God Please..."

"Are you ok?" a familiar voice asked.

She turned around and found Jake standing by. He was visibly concerned, but was not making any uninvited moves into her personal space. Though she had not seen him since their dramatic parting, none of that seemed to matter at this moment. She blurted out,

"I have to get the car...I have to go to the hospital...I feel like I can't breathe...I am so fucking scared..."

"Hey, slow down" he said stepping in and holding her up. "What happened?"

"It's Sophie...I think she's...I...I have to go there."

"Ok, ok, come on, I'll drive you down." She briefly thought this was probably not a good idea, but she didn't resist. She let him put a supporting arm around her and walk her all the way to The Farm.

"You don't have to drive me, Jake. I can take it from here." She said as he headed to the car.

"I know I don't. But I don't think it's wise for you to be driving all the way to the next town as emotional as you are."

She hesitated only slightly because he was right. She was still shaking and in all honesty she did not want to be alone.

"Ok"

At the hospital, she met Lissette outside Sophie's room.

"She's sleeping"

"Oh, thank God! I thought..."

"She collapsed. Suddenly lost consciousness. So I called the ambulance. Doctor says there is a possibility of metastasis to the brain."

"Oh, my goodness!" Although Lissette was remaining as professional as possible, Beth could sense her worry. "Pastor Burt?"

"Was here all night. He just went to freshen up at the house"

"Her Dad?" Lissette shook her head looking away and quietly added "But truth be told, he doesn't know just how bad it is"

"I don't understand"

"No one has told him. We've been sworn to secrecy. As far as I know, Burt and I are the only ones that know the full truth" Lissette turned to look Beth straight in the eye, "And now, you!"

A nurse came up and interrupted them. "Excuse me," said Lissette never taking her unwavering gaze off Beth until she and the nurse turned and went into Sophie's room. Beth watched for a while as they attended to their sleeping patient. Despite her condition, Sophie exuded beauty as she slept. But Beth felt it. There was something not settled. Something tugging at her. Something she was here to do. Sophie had brought sense back to her life when everything made none, now it was time for Beth to return the favor.

"I hear you, sister" Beth whispered, turned around and walked out of the hospital to the car where Jake was waiting.

"How is she?"

"I think she is waiting for something"

"Huh?"

"I think I've been called to do something"

"Oookay...I am sure you know what you are talking about. Where're we heading?"

"Home! Thanks so much, Jake. I've been meaning to tell you that. Thank you for being with me when I was at my lowest. Thank you for making me feel beautiful again. Thanks for making me feel good." He was looking at her like she was a little out of it, but she continued, "Of course I know now that it wasn't really *you*, it was me all along, but you held up a mirror for me in the time we spent together and it helped start me on the journey back to myself. And I thank you for that. And I am sorry about the mess along the way. I didn't mean to toy with your emotions or disrespect you. I think you are such an awesome young man and I foresee a beautiful and a deserving woman for you in the future. And you are both going to make each other very, very happy."

"Wow! Er…thanks?...And you? Will you be happy?"

She laughed, "Yes Jake, I will be happy. Come on, I've got work to do"

17

"Sister Bethany?!?!"

Sister Celia, the receptionist at the Blessed Jordan Evangelical Church stared at Beth in disbelief.

Beth had become so used to her new look, it had not occurred to her that most people had not yet seen her this way. This response to her appearance though flattering, was somewhat unnerving; she could not remember when last a woman looked at her as though she were a worthy rival for male attention. She almost faltered. Maybe this was not such a good idea after all? She could still leave with little damage done if she walked out right now. But a new inside voice spoke up and reminded her that running was no longer a part of who she was. It was time to own her choices and her actions. She would no longer *let* things happen. It was time to *make* things happen.

"Yes," She responded shyly "It's me"

"I almost didn't recognize you, you look amazing. Look at your hair and you've lost some weight too." Sister Celia's eyes wandered up and down Beth and then focused on her face mischievously as she asked, "What happened to you?"

No doubt the church had been gossiping. Beth ignored the question and asked to see the pastor.

Somewhat disappointed, Sister Celia looked back at her computer screen searching the pastor's calendar.

"He is really busy today. He is expecting some very important people in the next few minutes. I am not sure if he can see you today. Would you like me to check the rest of the week?"

"No, this is urgent! I need to see him today. Right now, would be ideal."

"Well, I cannot perform miracles and create more time on his calendar, you know" Sister Celia was curt and was not going to make this easy. It seemed best to play into whatever thoughts she was harboring about Beth's sudden and new reappearance.

"Could you just tell him that Sister Bethany is here with a crisis on her hands? I am sure you understand." She feigned an embarrassed look before turning away awkwardly.

It seemed to be working. In her peripheral vision, she could see Sister Celia studying her, obviously trying to figure out what the 'crisis' might be. Perhaps she could be the first to tell the ladies what had actually happened to handsome brother Cal's marriage. Beth jumped at this opportunity and placed her hand on her stomach suggestively. Sister Celia caught it. She stood up.

"Um, I'll see what he says, but I am not making any promises,"

Beth thanked her and smiled sheepishly, "I am sure you'll be able to convince him"

Sister Celia hurried into the pastor's office.

It didn't take long before she came back out smiling and put an encouraging hand on Beth's shoulder.

"He is just finishing up on a phone call. Don't worry, Sister Beth. He will see you now"

Sophie was quite the spitting image of her father. His height, his complexion and even at his age, that same smooth skin. His gray hair added a look of wisdom and dignity to his oozing power and charisma. His presence filled the room and made you feel like you truly might meet God.

"Pastor Rivers," She held out her hand and he took it.

"Good to see you Sister Bethany, it's been a while" She had never been this close to him. His charm was magnetic. Her hand seemed to melt in his and her body and mind followed. His dark eyes seemed to bore deep into her soul as if he could see and know everything about her. She could understand his power over Sophie.

"I…er…I…" she stumbled, working hard to overcome the fear that was rising within her, "Thank you…er…for seeing me at such short notice"

"I am always here for my flock," He smiled leading her to a chair, "what can I do for you?"

She accepted the seat, but sat up straight and tall to maintain any inkling of courage she had left.

"Well, um, I have a good friend who is dying."

"I am sorry to hear that." It was clearly not what he had expected. He took a seat opposite her.

"Yes, she is the most beautiful, most wonderful person I have ever met. We only just became friends, but already we know and trust each other so much. Like it was meant to be." He nodded with sympathy, his intense stare never wavering. She continued,

"The problem is she is dying. I have had to face the fact that there is no stopping it. I hoped and prayed, but then I had to make peace with it the same way she had done. She will not be with us much longer. It's like she is fading. Soon the image will be gone."

"What can I do to help you?" He probably heard these stories all the time, Beth thought, but his concern appeared genuine.

"To help *her*, actually"

"Of course! She needs prayer? Is she a Christian?"

"She is a Christian and yes, I am sure that she would welcome prayer. But more than anything, I feel she may need a father. Could you be that for her?"

"As a pastor it is my duty. Take me to her"

"I can't!" He was taken aback. So far everything had gone quite well and even though Beth now began to second guess herself it was too late to back out, "She will eventually know that I brought you to her, but I don't want it to be obvious when you walk in. You'll have to go alone. But you *must* go. The time is very short."

"Sister Bethany," He spoke slowly watching her suspiciously, "If there is a person in need, I will go. However, it does not sound like this person is very keen on my visit, so if you want me to see this person, you will have to go with me."

"Oh, she is keen! She has asked for you. She is just too scared to ask you herself."

"She is in this congregation?"

"She has been, yes." Beth could no longer stand the intensity of his eyes piercing through her so she proceeded to search in her bag for a paper she had come prepared with.

He watched her in silence.

Paper in hand now, she stood up and held it out to him,

"This is the information"

He stood up and keeping a close eye on her, took the paper and read it.

"What kind of joke is this?" He looked at her with fiery eyes and she felt like a naughty child.

"I felt it was my duty to let you know. She would never tell you herself. She is too scared of letting you down again. She thinks that dying would be letting you down. She's scared, but she needs you so bad." Beth rushed what she said, trying to get it all in before he had the chance to silence her.

"Sister Bethany, I think you should leave now." He said deliberately.

"I just… " she started, but he held up his hand,

"No! You need to leave right now. Celia!!!"

Sister Celia, who had obviously been listening at the door the whole time, came rushing in and ushered Beth out.

Walking out of the building, a wave of guilt washed over Beth. Had she really done the right thing or at least what was best for Sophie? After all, how could *she* determine what was best? What if she had now caused more trouble than help? Oh no! Not now when Sophie needed peace not turmoil.

She sat in her car across the street where she had parked, trying to reason with herself when she saw Pastor Rivers and another man rushing out of the church to his black Escalade. In hiding, she sat and watched the SUV. Pastor Rivers got into the back and the man, apparently his driver, got into the driver's seat. The brake lights came on with the engine and the SUV sped off down the street, barely catching the first seconds of a red light.

"I guess you get away with running red lights as a Pastor" Beth said out loud. She had a fair idea of what his rush might be and now dreaded Sophie's response.

"Well, what's done is done", she took a deep breath and sighed, "Time for round two!"

It had been almost four months since she had sped out of this driveway giving Cal the finger.

Now coming back she could feel the definite shift within her.

She was finally prepared to face Cal and yet, seeing that his car was not in the driveway, she felt relieved.

She let herself in the front door and took in the familiar smell of home. Home. The home they had built together, the home they had loved. It was strangely quiet and neat.

She took a walk round the living room. It seemed as though everything was exactly as she had left it. Nothing was out of place.

He must not spend much time down here, she thought as she fluffed a pillow.

The kitchen looked the same, untouched. No dirty dishes, no used glass on the counter. Perhaps her absence had forced him to clean up after himself or maybe he had hired a cleaning service.

She took the envelope of divorce papers from her tote, pulled out a letter she had prewritten and read it over.

"Dear Cal, I am setting you free!

For what it's worth, you were right. I should not have run. I should have stayed and talked it through with you. But I have been awakened from my self-focused slumber and I realize that we each have our own journey.

And so I set you free to take yours. And I set out on a new one of mine.

Thank you for everything.

I love you

Bethany

P.S. I have turned my phone back on. You can call me if we need to discuss legalities."

This was it, she thought. This was the beginning of a whole new life. Without Cal. The thought caused her heart to ache, but if he wanted to leave, she had to let him go.

She displayed the envelope neatly on the kitchen counter where he would not miss it, and after one last look around, she left quickly, knowing fully well that she was in fact, running away again.

At least he could call her now if he wanted, she thought as she quickly started the engine and drove back to Dunham.

Days passed and she had to admit to herself that she was hoping he would call. But he never did. It almost felt like she was losing him all over again, but this time it was for real. Cal was gone. She would have to focus on reconnecting with Stoney and that would have to be that.

She called Stoney a few times, but he never picked up and he didn't call back.

She sat beside Sophie's hospital bed riddled with guilt. She was losing everyone and she had brought it all on herself.

"It's not your fault you know" Sophie's feeble voice came out of the blue.

"What?" Beth jumped.

"Whatever you are thinking, it's not your fault."

"How do you know I was thinking anything at all?"

"It's written all over your face."

"You know, I hate that you can read me so well."

"No, you don't" Sophie laughed weakly.

"Do you need anything? Are you comfortable? Are you in pain or anything?"

Sophie shook her head.

"Listen," she said quietly, "I know you called my Dad."

Beth maintained a straight face, not registering any response.

Sophie reached out a hand and Beth took it.

"Thank you!" she smiled squeezing Beth's hand. "Thank you so much. It was the missing piece of the puzzle. I thought I was never going to find this peace beyond understanding they talk about. But I did. And I have you to thank. It's real, Beth. It's really real. And it's amazing. You were right, Beth. I had to open myself to it and once I did, I realized it had been there all along."

"I am so happy for you, Sophie."

"I want you to have it too, Beth. Promise me you will try. Don't be like me. Don't wait till all your time is gone. Do it now, while there is time to enjoy that peace. Promise me!"

Beth wasn't quite sure what it was Sophie was asking her to do, so she said nothing and only smiled and nodded.

Sophie was not convinced, "It's Love, Beth! Just open yourself to Love. Promise me!"

"I promise" Beth whispered.

Sophie's room was filled with flowers and paintings and the people she loved the most, her husband, her father, Lissette and Bethany.

The doctor looked up, "She's gone."

Pastor Rivers jumped forward in protest, "Well, bring her back, do something"

Lissette put a reassuring hand on his arm, "She had a DNR in place, Pastor! She was ready!"

The grieving father looked searchingly at the doctor who only nodded in agreement and then this force of nature, this man whose presence could quieten a storm, collapsed into the chair next to Sophie and wept, moaning and groaning, his elegant shoulders shaking with his sobs.

Burt stared motionless.

Beth was rendered speechless by the huge lump in her throat. She looked around the room in a daze. The brightly colored flowers, the paintings, the cards, the warm rays of sunlight streaming through the window over Sophie who reflected every bit of the brightness and beauty of her surroundings as she lay silently and forevermore sleeping. Sophie went the way she'd wanted. Surrounded by light and love. This beautiful angel had returned to her heavenly home.

Beth swallowed hard. Her throat was beginning to hurt as the lump grew and stretched.

"You okay?" Lissette whispered.

"Yes, yes thanks. I need to step outside"

Beth walked out of the room leaving the grieving men with Sophie and headed out to her car.

Once outside, she began to breathe deeply forcing air into her extremely tight chest. She was certain that a good cry would relieve the pressure, yet for all the physical pain she felt, she could shed no tears. Emotionally, she felt numb.

She started the car and drove back to The Farm in complete silence, musing the whole time at what a beautiful day it was. She was not certain if the sun had shone this golden in the last few weeks. Surely it was Sophie adding her glow.

Walking through her front garden at The Farm, she stretched out her arms and lifted her head, letting the warm glow of the early evening sun wash over her. She walked slowly by her flowers, admiring each one as she walked by. Did flowers know when people died?

She let herself in the front door and looked around the room. Sophie was everywhere.

She willed herself to cry with no success.

She gave up and went up the stairs, threw herself onto the bed and fell asleep.

18

It had been three days and still the sun cast its bright golden glow over Bethany's flowers.

Still Beth had not cried.

Still she remained numb.

She avoided the living room as much as possible.

Every day she would sit outside in the sun on the apple tree stump watching as bees visited the colorful blossoms in her now vibrant garden. She watched spiders spinning their webs between stems and leaves as the gentle breeze swayed everything this way and that.

Then she would go indoors and lay on her bed staring at the ceiling until she fell asleep again.

She heard a car stop outside and then heard the gate open. There was some indistinct conversation.

Then a knock at the door. Silence. Then another. And another.

She got up lacking interest or curiosity and went downstairs to open the front door.

"Sister Bethany"

She stood aghast trying to find the voice she just realized she had not used at all in three days.

"Pastor Rivers!"

He stood at her front door, his driver behind him carrying some packages wrapped in brown paper.

His loss had not softened his eyes. Still they bored through her pulling at her soul like a hook.

"You left these paintings at the hospital," he indicated the driver, "Lisette told me where to find you so I could return them."

"Those paintings belonged to Sophie. So you can keep them."

"That's kind of you. I am happy to accept them" He responded with an air of formality. There was an awkward moment of silence as they stood in the doorway, each waiting for the other to speak first.

"May I come in?" he asked eventually.

She made no attempt to hide her hesitation but he was undaunted.

"Er, yes, okay, I guess" She said stepping aside for him.

Pastor Rivers signaled for the driver to take the packaged paintings back to the car and then he stepped past her into the living room. Beth closed the door behind him and leaned against it folding her arms in front of her chest.

He said nothing but just stood where he was and looked around the room.

He turned to her and seemed to ask for permission to move around. She nodded.

He slowly began to move around the room closely examining every painting and every picture of Sophie.

"I see" he said several times. She did not respond. "You are good"

"I had a good subject." She replied still leaning against the door. "Her life just jumps out at you when you are painting. It's easy to paint a good subject"

He seemed to chuckle "Even as a child. So full of life you couldn't contain her." He moved to the next picture.

"I failed her!" he said quietly.

Beth heard him, but remained silent as though she hadn't.

He went on, speaking louder now.

"Ephesians 6:2, Honor your father and mother so that it may be well with you and that you may live long on the earth." he stared at the painting in front of him, "She honored me. She fulfilled my dream. Never spoke back, never rebelled. Did all that was expected of her."

He moved to a photograph pinned to the wall, "Love your neighbors, love your enemies…It goes without saying that you love your children. It's natural. But I failed her."

A pause, then a deep breath. "She cared so much for me, but I cared only for myself. My own daughter couldn't come to me when she was in pain. Couldn't tell me she was dying. Couldn't share her suffering with me. Not because she didn't want to. But because I had treated her in such a way that she felt she couldn't."

Beth felt extremely uncomfortable. What was he expecting from her? Was she supposed to join him in his blame game and reaffirm his failure? Or was he expecting reassurance?

She remained quiet.

"Hebrews 13:2" he continued, "Be not forgetful to entertain strangers: for thereby some have entertained angels unawares. I didn't! I didn't entertain the angel that God had planted in my own home. Didn't value her. So He took her. Her life was not cut short because of anything *she* did, but because of what *I* didn't do. He took her from me, just like He took her mother. I failed…again."

There was no mistaking the quiver in his voice but Beth had no idea what she was supposed to say.

"…and yet, she was so forgiving that even on her death bed, she could forgive me and love me in my shame and guilt. She hugged me and loved me and forgave me."

Silence!

Beth shifted a little and cleared her throat. He took a breath and turned around suddenly.

He looked at Beth and spoke in a very controlled voice,

"She told me about your work and about 'Epiphany'. She believed in it."

"I am so honored" Beth replied hoping it was the right thing to say.

"She set aside funding and it was her wish that we sponsor you."

"I…excuse me?" She stood up straight.

"I know nothing about art shows, so it's up to you to make it happen, but I will see to it that all your expenses are covered. And if you need any help at all, we will provide it."

"I don't know what to say"

"You brought her so much joy in these last days. She said you were like the sister she never had, the mother she lost, the lover I stole from her, all in one. You made quite an impact."

"She did the same for me."

"Forty-six years under my very nose, but it took you to help me *see* her and *know* her when she had only days left. Without you, I would have had only a phone call saying she was gone. I am…grateful…for those last moments I was able to share with her" Beth could see his struggle. This was clearly hard for him.

"I only did what I thought was right."

He nodded, "She asked to be cremated and have her ashes scattered by the lake in Jefferson Park on a bright and sunny day. It was her favorite picnic spot when she was little. And the last place she saw her mother. It will be a small and private service but you should be there. She would want that."

"Thank you. I would love to."

He moved uneasily, apparently getting ready to head out, then with his head hung low he added,

"Cremation isn't my thing but she said she was boxed in in life and demanded to be set free in death." he looked up at Beth, "It was me. I kept her in that box! And I'll be damned if I return her to a box. I will not fail her again!"

He strode with long strong steps and stood in front of her taking in her disheveled state.

"And now these three remain: Faith, Hope and Love. But the greatest of these is Love. That's from First Corinthians! Remember

Bethany, *Now* is all the time there is. And Love is always there. Accept it while you yet have life." She was struck by the fact the he called her by just her name. He still spoke in his stern manner, but she could feel some warmth. "I will keep you informed about the memorial"

"Yes, please! Thank you"

"And you will keep me informed about preparations for the show. Burt can help you"

"Yes, thank you again. I will put some thought into it once I get myself back together somehow."

"Now is all the time there is!" He repeated watching her closely, then he opened the door, said "God bless you." and was gone.

Standing where he had left her, she looked around the room as if it had all been a dream.

She looked at her work. Epiphany! She remembered how it all came about. She remembered the moments she had captured in photographs. Remembered living those moments. Remembered the words shared in those moments. She smiled. It had been a wonderful time. Pastor Rivers' words rang in her head *"Now is all the time there is…"* She remembered Sophie's happy face after she had reconciled with her father *"Open yourself up to the love…" "do it now while you have the time to enjoy the peace…"*

"Now is all the time there is…" "Love is always there…"

The words went round and round in her head until she almost felt dizzy. And then she knew. She understood. She remembered. She, and only she, was in control of what happened next. *She* would have to make the decision to continue. Only she, and not someone else could love herself enough to move on to the next greatest thing that God and Life had in store for her.

Right there and then, the decision was made.

She bounded up the stairs, freshened up, put on a tank top and leggings and went out for a run.

The fresh air filled her lungs as she ran. She saw Jake working in a garden and waved to him, he just stared back at her. She yelled "Have a great day" to the old lady selling vegetables and the lady waved back smiling. She took in all the beauty that was around her. Getting to Main Street, she stopped and quietly watched for a moment. People were all about their business hustling and bustling. She smiled at a man passing by with his dog and he nodded in return.

Nothing had stopped, life was still happening, and she was a part of it.

She was a part of Life!

"Yes, I am!" she said out loud, "I am a part of Life!"

19

"At first I was jealous of you. For years I was Sophie's best friend, now suddenly in a matter of weeks here you were, stealing my position. She was always talking about you. It bothered the heck out of me, but it was quickly clear that you needed to be there. I wasn't there. But you were."

Burt smiled at her in the dim light of the Capital Grille Restaurant. He had invited her to dinner to go over some suggestions for possible venues for her show. In the weeks since Sophie had been set free, Beth had worked diligently on completing her unfinished pieces. She lost track of time as she gave in to the flow if inspiration that seemed to have overcome her from the day she made the decision to live and love fully. This was the first time she was alone with Burt, and she was looking forward to the opportunity to get to hear his side of the stories Sophie had told.

"She said you were needed at the church."

"Yes, I know. She was intent on keeping me there. She was right of course, if I was going to stay in her father's good graces, I had to be at the church. She was always right. Always knew what was best for everyone else and willing to sacrifice herself for it."

"And did you succeed in staying in Pastor Rivers' good graces?" He looked surprised at her question so she went on, "Well, I mean, so you were there for the church, but you didn't tell him the truth about Sophie's condition. How did he take that?"

"Yeah! That was a close call, but like father like daughter, they have this amazing way of putting what makes sense above what they feel. They are incredibly strong. Sometimes I think their strength is their weakness. They could self-destruct"

"She very nearly did. I truly believe she was waiting for him."

"I think you are right."

"But honestly Burt, why didn't you tell him?"

"She made me promise not to. How could I betray her? I owe my whole life as I know it to her. I would give her whatever she wanted. She was so adamant about going this alone. Even when Lissette called me over the night she collapsed, we both tried to convince her to let us tell him, but she shut us down. It wasn't easy on either of us."

"I guess I can imagine. I am glad she never thought I would go tell him, because she might have vowed me to secrecy too. And I would just have had to break my vow"

He smiled, taking the hit, "I understand"

"I am sorry, that was cold." she paused. "You have known these people much longer than I have, I am in no position to judge you"

"But you are right" he took a gulp of his spritzer. "I should have taken a stand" he took another gulp. "I see why you two got along. You have that same stubborn strength, don't you?"

"Ha! Hardly!" she laughed. "I have managed to make a complete mess of a life that was going just fine thank you. And I have taken every wrong turn since then so that I can't go back. Maybe I *am* stubborn. It took long enough for me to even admit I wanted my life back. Stubborn? Yes. But strength? No way! I am a complete wuss!"

"But you *did* admit you want your life back…that admission still takes strength. Making wrong turns doesn't make you weak, it takes strength to make choices that you need to stand by. And talking to my father in law took strength too. Not to mention this show you are putting together…that takes courage. You are underestimating yourself."

"Well…I am just trying to be strong enough to lay in the bed I have made for myself without crying every night."

"Sophie would hate to hear you talk like this."

"Yes, she would"

"And she would do something about it"

"Yes, she would. She would whoop me upside the head!"

They both laughed.

"Maybe she still will." He looked at his watch, "Hey listen, I need to go make a call. Go ahead and order if you like. They already know to put everything on my account"

"No, it's Ok. I'll wait for you."

She sat waiting patiently for him to return and was just beginning to wonder what had happened to him when a man approached the table from behind her and stopped next to it.

"Excuse me" he said and she recognized his voice at once. It still had same effect on her as it did years ago when she would sit trans-fixed listening to all his thoughts on politics; when she went to sleep at night dreaming of his voice; when she would call him up just to hear him say 'Hello'.

There was no avoiding him, he was here, right here beside her.

Slowly, she looked up at him. Scanning him from the well-pol-ished shoes up his muscular legs softly covered by his deep gray suit pants. There he stood. Tall, slender and still perfect!

He had grown a short beard, speckled with grey. He looked charmingly debonair. His beautiful dark eyes sparkled as they stared at her in shocked amazement. Any remaining doubt about her feel-ings for him, was completely gone. Right now, in this moment, all she wanted to do was jump into his arms.

"Bethany?" he could barely speak.

"Hi Cal" she said softly, and smiled at him.

"What the.…What..I mean, Hi!…I mean, what are you doing here?" he blurted, doing a really bad job of concealing his shock. She wasn't sure if she had ever seen him at such a loss of words. She responded calmly,

"Well, um, I was about to have dinner with Pastor Burt but he just stepped away to make a call"

His blubbering continued, "Oh Ok! That's nice! Damn Beth! You look stunning! Your hair! You cut it, it looks so good and my God, just look at you. I can't believe I am seeing you, it's been so long and I am just here to meet…Wait a minute, you're having dinner with Pastor Burt? Burt, Pastor Burt?"

"Well, yeah!" She rolled her eyes.

"Oh, I see!" He looked around for Burt and then back at her, obviously having found his wits again. She smiled up at him silently. His usual suave self had returned, but with an extreme twist of humility in the mix.

"I have missed you so much! I have practiced this moment over and over again, praying that I could just have a chance to see you and talk to you. Could I sit?"

"Of course you can, Cal" Unlike Cal, she had not practiced this moment over and over. She was just playing it by ear and going with the flow. One thing she was sure of, was that she was happy to see him, and whatever he was about to say, she wanted to hear it, if only to keep him here longer.

He sat across from her and looked at her with so much intensity, she blushed. When they were dating, he used to get a kick out of making her blush. She expected he would tease her about it, but he only said,

"It's really good to see you."

"It's really great to see you too." she smiled. "I love the new look. It suits you."

He chuckled. "Glad you like it. I didn't grow it intentionally at first. Just wasn't shaving"

"Oh, ok" She shrugged.

"I don't know why I am so nervous. I just…Beth I know it just sounds like words, but I honestly mean it when I say I am so sorry that I hurt you. I am sorry that I went with Marla. I am sorry that I let other feelings cloud my judgment. I don't know how many ways I can say it or prove it to you, but I deeply regret my actions." He searched her for a reaction but got none, "I have missed you so much. My life is incomplete without you. You are my best friend. How could I have risked that? I see you here now and I just feel like I don't want to let you out of my sight again…ever! I just don't want to ever not see you again. I don't want to not hear your voice even if you're nagging. I don't want to live without you. One life is all we get and I want to spend my one life with you." She stared at him, speechless. "I know, I know, you've moved on and you are obviously happier without me, but I have been begging God for a chance to at least be able to tell you how I feel, even if I can't win you back." He reached for her hand and she let him take it. "I love you Beth. I still, and always will, love you."

His words were hitting the spot but Beth was apprehensive,

"Win me back? But you sent divorce papers?"

"That was just a cheap trick. I was hoping it would shock you into coming back to me."

"But I signed them."

"You did?"

"I signed them and brought them back to the house. I left them on the kitchen table for you."

"You signed them? …so…you want the divorce?"

"I thought *you* did"

"And you granted it?"

"I left you a note. I said if you wanted to be with someone else, I would not hold you back. I gave you your freedom to be happy."

"My happiness is with you"

"What about Marla?"

"There is no Marla. There is no college. I took a leave of absence to get away from it all. And I haven't been home in forever. I didn't want to be there without you so I rented a small studio apartment overlooking the river, not too far from here. I have been spending a lot of time in solitude, and I have finally started writing the book I have talked about for years."

She stared at him, torn between confusion, disbelief and excitement

"That's why the house looked so empty?! And the divorce papers are still on the kitchen table?"

"They must be! And I guess I should let you know that Pastor Burt is not coming back. This is a set up."

"You set this up?"

"No, not me! After you left and I couldn't reach you and your mother got tired of having me over there whining all the time, I went for counseling with Pastor Burt. He helped me through it. It was he who suggested I get away, get started on something else, get my mind off things and feel good about myself again. He had me practice what I would say to you if I had the chance. And today, he called me up and invited me to dinner."

"Sophie!"

"Sister Sophie?"

"Yes, I guess you could say I was counselling with her. She helped me to prepare to face life without you, but she always knew that wasn't what I really wanted. She urged me to talk to you but I was so certain you had moved on. I never called."

"You counseled with Sister Sophie? But how?"

"It's a long story but she probably put Burt up to this. Bless you Sophie, you crazy girl! Listen Cal, I have some things I want to say too. And I need us to be clear with each other before we go any further" He nodded and she went on,

"I am sorry I hurt you too. I probably shouldn't have run off the way I did and stayed away from everyone for so long. But in a way, I am glad I did. I learned a lot about myself and about life. I am not the same woman I used to be."

"I can see that" he smiled admiringly at her.

"And, um, I, um, I met someone and I, er, well I had a fling with him." She saw shock and anger register on Cal's face as he pulled his hand away sitting back.

"It was nothing serious," she added quickly, "It was very short but sweet, and it gave me a better understanding of what you probably went through." He remained silent. "It also totally messed up my relationship with Stoney."

"Oh? How so?"

"Well, he walked in on us and found out the truth about our separation, since you hadn't told him."

Cal sighed, "So *that's* why he's been giving me the cold shoulder. He stopped talking to me completely. Won't answer my calls, never calls me back."

"You made me the bad guy, Cal. Not very nice! You should have told him the truth"

"I thought you were coming back! Thought I could keep the whole thing quiet until we sorted it out. And how come he knew where to find you anyway?"

"Mom. I told her she could tell him"

"Oh, really?"

"He's my child, Cal! And he didn't cheat on me!"

"I suppose I have to accept that"

"Then I met Sophie as she was dying and we had the most amazing time together that I will forever be grateful for. I learned so much from her. In the time I spent with her I grew up, I opened up, I released, I was reborn. She didn't require anything of me. She didn't tell me what I must do, or who I must be and in that short time before she died...I found me."

"I never told you what to do or who to be, Beth! I loved you just the way you were" He argued.

"You are right, Cal! But I had to see that for myself. In my mind, I thought I had to be a certain kind of wife to you and it was draining me fitting myself into that mold. But now I know that it was me who created the mold, not you! And now I know...and I am sure... that I want to spend the rest of my life with you," She tried to reach for him but he held back. "...if you still want me"

He ran his hand over his face and sat looking out of the window. She knew it would be hard for him to accept her affair with Jake, but she had decided on total honesty. She would not get back with Cal and harbor such a secret. It would inevitably become a problem between them.

Giving him time to work through it, she continued talking about herself.

"I rediscovered my soul. I went back to my Art. I have a living room full of paintings and drawings and Sophie, her father and Burt are sponsoring my first show." Cal showed some interest, but was obviously still preoccupied. She went on, "I rediscovered my body. I listen to it speak to me and I take care of it. I know what I am feeling and I don't deny it. I don't run from my feelings anymore. And I am not running away from saying what I mean anymore either. I am not running away at all anymore, Cal. I am owning myself now. I am not being anyone else but me anymore or ever again. All my cards are on the table."

He watched her with skepticism. She took a sip of her wine to mask her disappointment at his reaction while reassuring herself that she was doing the right thing. She remembered how Sophie had said that total honesty in her relationship was difficult. Now she could see how. But it had worked for Sophie and Burt, would it work for her?

Cal shifted in his seat and leaned forward over the table.

"I agree with everything. I mean, I thought we were always authentic, I have always been me."

"Maybe you, but it wasn't that way for me. I lost myself in everybody else's life. It was never about me. Everything was always for someone else. It's about me now."

"And it should be. I want it to be. I want to give you what you want. I want to make you happy."

"No Cal, I have to be happy in myself. It's not your job to make me happy."

"I get it, Oprah!" he scoffed.

"Cal, I'm being serious"

"Beth, Listen! It's great that you have made all these self-discoveries and that you have come into your own the way you have. It was something you felt you needed and it makes you a better person. That's great, I am proud of you for that. But I am *not* happy about the idea of you with some other guy and I can't promise that this is not going to be a problem between us, I mean this is really fucking with me right now."

"Hey, now hold on a minute…" Beth was about ready to remind him how this whole thing got started in the first place, but he stopped her,

"No, no, let me finish before you get all heated. You've had time to digest the whole Marla thing, I'm only just hearing about dude now, so it's hard for me,"

He did have a point there, she thought as half of her just wanted to kneel down and beg for his forgiveness and the other half stood with a *'yeah and'* look on her face and her arms folded.

She remembered her reaction when she had found out about him. She had walked out. Would he do the same?

Cal continued, "Listen, it's not easy and it's not going to be easy, I don't know what's going to happen in our future but I'm asking myself is it worth it to let you go again? And I don't want to. Now is all the time there is, I have you here with me now. I want us to fix this."

"What did you just say?"

"I want us to fix this"

"No, before that"

"The other guy?"

"No, silly, you said 'Now is all the time there is'. Where did you get that?"

"It's just the truth, isn't it?..." as Cal began to philosophize about the illusion of time she heard the echo of Pastor Rivers' voice *'Now is all the time there is and Love is always there. Accept it while you yet have life'* Could Pastor Rivers himself have been a part of this set up as well? What did it matter? Here was Cal, the man she had always loved, saying he wanted to fix it. Is this not what she had longed for? Was this not the answer to her prayers? Could this be real?

"Beth? Beth, what's up?" He noticed her drifting.

"Nothing...I was just remembering something...You know Cal, you are absolutely right. Now is all the time we have and we have a lot of fixing to do, so why don't we just go home and make love?" she was startled and amused at her own boldness, but what was there to lose at this point?

He stared at her in shocked silence for a few seconds. He hadn't expected that. His brow furrowed as he seemingly scrutinized every feature in her face. She smiled, nervous. He sighed, looked down and shook his head.

Well, so much for that, she was just saying to herself when he stood up, came round the table to stand beside her, reached out his hand to her and asked, "Your place or mine?"

Though his hesitation was clear, she recognized that unmistakable change in his voice now heavy with desire. Oh, how she had missed that.

She ran her hand up his thigh stopping just short of his crotch before placing it in his. Then she stood right in front of him, raised her hand to his face and let it trace his jawline while leaning in as if to kiss him. He leaned forward not initiating but ready for the kiss, but she just let her lips touch his lightly before she whispered, "Sex by the river sounds pretty fabulous, don't you think?"

Then, keeping her eyes locked on his, she let her hand slide down his chest and abs once again stopping just short of his now very invigorated crotch. She smiled and moved by him letting her body rub against him just enough as she turned to towards the exit, her inner vixen rejoicing.

"I kinda like this new Beth." Cal smiled and followed.

20

"Babe?" came Cal's voice from downstairs, "Are you ready yet? Stoney is already on his way there, we need to go." "Coming" she yelled back, as she examined herself in the mirror one last time. She stood tall in her silver Jimmy Choo pumps. Her off the shoulder black lace dress clung to her now slender and toned body, her short hair revealing her graceful neck and shoulders. She donned a pair of silver drop earrings Cal had presented her with to celebrate this occasion. She could hardly believe that she was the same woman who not too long ago stood before this very same mirror feeling ugly, frustrated, hurt and worthless. Yet here she stood, confident, proud, madly in love with herself and with life and not feeling in the least guilty that the living room had not been vacuumed and that there was a load of laundry piled up in the laundry room.

After their initial reconciliation at the restaurant, 'Sex by the river' had actually turned out to be a serious conversation about their relationship and the direction each of them wanted to go as individuals and as a couple. It had started over a glass of wine while sitting on the balcony of his studio overlooking the river. The gentle sound of the gurgling water filled the angry silences between yells and curses. The first night they lay together, the next, she chose to sleep on the pull out sofa alone. The following night they barely got any sleep at all. Several times he had lost his temper and several times she had almost walked out again. Finally, they were back in each other's arms tired of fighting and wholly surrendered to the veracity that they earnestly wanted to stay together and would, no matter what.

Afterwards, she had taken him to The Farm and introduced him to her work. This was a part of Beth he had never known so it took him quite by surprise and he found it mindboggling that she could have kept it stifled inside her for so long. "You think you know a person…" he kept mumbling as he walked around the house.

Everything else seemed to fall into place naturally after that.

They drove out to one of Stoney's concerts and surprised him back stage. He beamed like a child at Christmas when he saw them together. There were hugs, tears, apologies, love and laughter all round as they talked through the family's last few months over a late night IHOP dinner that turned into an early morning break-fast. It was an added bonus that they in fact truly enjoyed the show, dancing freely alongside the screaming millennials. They beamed with pride as Cal told anyone within earshot that his son was re-sponsible for the interactive installments that made up the back-drop of the entire dance party.

Her mother welcomed them back with a huge smile, a warm hug and lots of food. "I told you to be patient" she smiled at Cal, "I knew she'd be back."

Beth smiled at herself in the mirror, "You've come a long way, baby" she said as she picked up her silk shawl, turned out the light and hur-ried down the stairs.

Cal looked up at her on the stairs and smiled.

"Do I look as nervous as I feel?" she asked.

"Not at all. You look absolutely gorgeous!"

Stoney was waiting to meet them in the parking lot. He cleaned up really nicely, she thought to herself as she admired him in his dark suit.

"Oh honey, you look so handsome! I am so happy you are here" She gave him a hug.

"What? I wouldn't miss this for the world, Mom. I am so proud of you on so many levels"

"Please don't make me cry yet, my make-up will run and I still need to make a half way decent speech."

"You'll do great, Mom".

"I keep telling her that" Cal chimed in.

"Come on, we'd better get inside, Grandma is all nervous about your being late. She's been here for twenty minutes already"

"Yeah, well, you know your Grandma." said Beth locking each of her arms into that of each of her favorite men on either side. She took a deep breath "Come on, boys!"

Heading into the hall, she smiled brightly as she read the sign that adorned the entrance:

Hillman Gallery Presents Sophie's Epiphany! - An Introspective featuring the works of Bethany Clarice Lambeau

Beth stood at the podium looking out at the audience applauding her. She saw the familiar faces of the people that had got her here - her parents, her husband, her son, Pastor Burt, Pastor Rivers and Lissette.

The piece called '*Sunlight*' stood beside her on the stage showing Sophie in all her glory, with her head thrown back in laughter, wearing a wide brimmed summer hat surrounded by the radiance of the sun. The entire painting was done in shades of orange and yellow.

The applause stopped and the audience waited politely for her to begin speaking.

But if there was one thing the last months had taught her, it was to slow down and take in the moment. She breathed deeply and searched herself for a definition of what she was experiencing in this amazing moment and she found it. She recognized it. It was a familiar feeling from a time before time. Not because of her husband or her son, not because she had been given her first art show, not because there was a room full of people applauding her. Not because life appeared perfect right now. That was false. Nothing and no one was perfect. And searching for perfection was futile, she now knew. No, it was not in the perfection but in the imperfection that she found it.

It was in herself that she found it and she knew what it was.

In this very moment, she felt Love.

In this very moment, she felt Joy.

In this very moment, even in the midst of uncertainty, she knew that she had finally found what she had been seeking - Peace! Everything didn't have to be in its perfect place for there to be peace. She just had to breathe and release. Accept what was before her and love it anyway. Accept herself and love herself anyway. Accept life and love life anyway.

Sophie had been right about everything.

She turned to the portrait of Sophie and said "Thank you, my friend."

Then she turned to the audience and began her speech.

THE END

ACKNOWLEDGEMENTS

Dear Reader, I must beg your pardon for the length of this section, but since this is my first book, it is imperative that I make mention of the substantial number of people who played a role in its creation and in bringing me to the place in my life where I am able to create thus.

First and foremost, a very special thank you to you, The Reader! Thank you for welcoming me into your space and allowing me to accompany you on this entertaining journey through emotion, thought, and words.

A BIG thank you to the GUBU Writers Group:
Bathsheba Cohen, Andrea Lewis, Yolanda Moore, Dannyelle Burton, Nickisha Bennett-Burton, Glenniver Sargeant.
This book got started because we got started! This is it, Ladies!!!
Special mention to Yoyo because...you know why!

Thank you to my first readers:
Sara Obregon, Dr. Ifeyinwa Adegbulugbe, Dr. Posi Odusote, Kevin Neil Bernard,
Karin Meessen, Anette Dowideit, Conswalia Green.
You gave me the courage to believe in this story.

Thank you to Marina Alfano:
No, Marla is not you, but you *are* a gorgeous Argentine Goddess.
Your enthusiastic help and encouragement mean so much to me.

Thank you to Segun Oguntola:
Our time together is so limited, yet so enriching.
Your encouragement and advice took me from fear to action.

Thank you to Dr. Conrad Cathcart:
You started me on my journey out of the dark;
Bringing me to this awesome and fearless point in my life.
I am forever grateful.

Thank you to My Families:
Olupitan and all its extensions through marriage, Berek, Ijalana, Broomes, Wilson.
The love and joy of being a part of these families always puts a smile on my face
and makes every day worth living.
Special mention to Alero and Patrick because…you know why!

Thank you to my husband, Clayton Broomes Jr.:
For the invaluable guidance on storytelling, for letting me be me, and for being patient while I work through my own personal journey with its many twists and turns.
Thank you for always urging me to be my best.

Last but by no means least, thank you to my boys,
Christian and Sebastian.
Being your mother opens me up to priceless opportunities to become my ultimate best self.
I love you!

ABOUT THE AUTHOR

The daughter of a German mother and a Nigerian father, Susan Olupitan grew up in Nigeria. She received her Dental Degree at the College of Medicine of the University of Lagos. After immigrating to America, Susan pursued her dream of becoming an actor.

Susan's love for stories of all kinds shifted her focus from performing to writing. She is married to writer/director Clayton Broomes Jr. and has two sons. *It Takes Water* is her debut novel.

Made in the USA
Middletown, DE
19 July 2019